A MAN FOR TOMORROW

Craig Fisher had received a visit from a Mr. Morgan from the Home Office, who had told him a most unlikely tale. But Fisher could not ignore it, and he found himself setting out to meet a people from the stars who had declared that they would talk only with him. He was taken to a haven in Greenland, where the aliens put their case to him. He agreed to make a journey to a dying world, but the purpose the aliens had for him was very different from what they had told him.

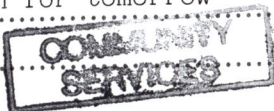

JAMES WALLACE

A MAN
FOR
TOMORROW

Complete and Unabridged

LINFORD
Leicester

First published in Great Britain in 1976 by
Robert Hale Limited
London

First Linford Edition
published 2003
by arrangement with
Robert Hale Limited
London

British Library CIP Data

Wallace, James
    A man for tomorrow.—Large print ed.—
Linford mystery library
    1. Detective and mystery stories
    2. Large type books
    I. Title
    823.9′14 [F]

ISBN 0–7089–4969–X

Published by
F. A. Thorpe (Publishing)
Anstey, Leicestershire

Set by Words & Graphics Ltd.
Anstey, Leicestershire
Printed and bound in Great Britain by
T. J. International Ltd., Padstow, Cornwall

This book is printed on acid-free paper

1

This author, the last paragraph of the review read, *can justly be said to have contributed more to contemporary interest in occult matters than any other. His style is simple and eminently readable, and he approaches even the most obscure and least definable of subjects in a lucid and practical manner. We have all learned much from him concerning those matters of life and death which are nearest to our secret hearts. More, please, Mr. Fisher!*

Craig Fisher laid his copy of the Newsman aside; then, placing his elbows on top of the desk before him, he cupped his chin in his hands and stared out of the window into the night. Gratifying, yes. When a critic of Dalton Becker's standing wrote such unrestrained words of praise, they had to mean a great deal. In fact they confirmed all the pleasant things which Fisher's fans had been writing to

1

him of late. Not to feel vain about it, he did believe that he had helped the man in the street to come to an understanding of true religion and the reason for living. He had achieved his aim; in that sense he was a success. But there were also the economic facts of life, and, no matter how pleased a man might feel with his work and himself, he ignored them at his peril.

His latest book, *The Talisman of Mu*, had taken a year to write, but looked like earning less than seven hundred pounds. It had been the same with *The Cults of Khem* and *The Wisdoms of Milarepa The Sage*, and his earlier books had brought him even smaller rewards. He could not go on like it. Whatever occupation a man pursued, the return on his efforts had to be sufficient to cover his needs and make a reasonable life possible. Failing that, his work was self-defeating and it was a mockery to continue it. Praise was good food for the ego, but it did nothing for the stomach; and, while talent might know itself fulfilled and the spirit feel justified, there was no substitute for money in the bank when the bills started rolling in. The fact was, he had been living at a deficit during these last seven years — or, perhaps more correctly, had been subsidising his work out of the few thousand pounds which his father had left him — but the money was now almost gone, and tonight he found himself forced to the final acceptance that he was never going to be even a reasonable success financially and that he would do well to get out of writing into a less glamorous but more lucrative occupation.

It was hard to be too objective about it, but he supposed last week's offer of a job from Tommy Stark had really been a godsend. It could even amount to a last chance to achieve some kind of recovery in life before it was too late. Last birthday he had become thirty seven years old. Now that was youngish or not so young, according to a person's outlook; but it was certainly late enough in the day for a man to start learning a new business. He was the more grateful as he considered the risk that Tommy Stark would be taking in him. Authors might be rather clever with words and ideas, but they were usually duds in commerce, and he feared that he might prove no exception to the rule. Yet Tommy was his oldest friend, knew him better than anybody else, and had expressed complete faith in him, so he realized that he must have faith in himself. Yes — there was nothing else for it — he would see Tommy in the morning and tell him that he was ready to jack in the writer's craft and enter the building supply industry. He would then do his damndest to learn and make himself worthy of his salt in the shortest possible time; but — it was going to be the hell of a change; and he suspected that the gap between the hidden meanings of the Song of Solomon and the cost of plumbing materials was going to prove even wider than he imagined.

Rising from his desk, Fisher picked up a thin sheaf of typescript and glanced down its top page. The work didn't read at all badly. *Inhabitants of Time* could well have been his best book to date. There was enough evidence in the Chronicles of Mu, the Rig Veda, Plato,

4

the Book of the Dead, and the Bible itself to indicate that Earth had been a regular stopover for the galaxy-skipping 'gods who were aforetime'. Those strange clairvoyant dreams that he had been having of spatial migrations and the seeding of worlds had also, he was convinced, had their place in the vista of life without end which he had seen it as his duty to pass on. Well, there were others who were at least as well equipped as he to do the work, and in the end nothing would be lost by his disappearance from that special corner of more than human knowledge to which only the spiritually advanced were summoned.

Opening the large drawer above the knee-hole of his desk — the one in which it had long been his habit to keep all new typescript — Fisher thrust away the sheaf of paper in his hand and banged the drawer shut on it. So much for his dreams and what the financially uninformed had jealously regarded as a promising career. It had been a trying day: one in which he had often stopped work and tried to match impossible solutions to an impossible situation. He could do with a drink; it wouldn't matter if the alcohol slowed him down or thickened his wits at this time of the day. He would drink to the past and salute the future in the same draught. Let the present hold the balance. He had done his best, and could only suppose that no more was required of him.

He walked to the sideboard, and was about to take the stopper out of the whisky decanter, when a knock sounded at the front door. He turned his head and glanced at the clock on the wall above the mantelpiece. Nine o'clock. Who could be calling on him this late in the evening? The position of his cottage — at the end of a rutted and none too salubrious lane, which separated it from the main road by some hundreds of winding yards — usually deterred all but familiar or previously announced visitors from coming to his home after dark. It could be Tommy Stark, he supposed; but Tommy had said nothing about calling round when they had parted in the Cleggburgh Bull last

Friday at lunchtime, for it had been tacitly understood that their next meeting would come through him, Fisher. Also, he had heard nothing of a car; and Stark would never walk down to the cottage. It was against his principles to walk anywhere that he didn't have to.

Leaving his work-cum-living room, Fisher walked through the gloom of the short hall beyond it and opened the front door on to a moon-streaked sky and flying droplets of rain. He could see so much of the night because his visitor was standing well back from the unlighted threshold. The other was male and presented a large and somewhat sinister shape. Certainly, he was a stranger, and Fisher felt no immediate inclination to invite him in. 'Yes?' he inquired.

'Mr. Fisher?' the other asked in polite and cultured tones.

'I am he.'

'My name is Morgan. Terence Morgan. I am from the Home Office. May I come in?'

'The Home Office?' Fisher was mystified. 'What on earth could anybody from the Home Office possibly want with me?'

'Quite a lot,' Morgan returned seriously, 'and most urgently. I am the Home Secretary's personal assistant. Perhaps it would help if you switched on a light and I showed you my identity card.'

Fisher moved out on to the doorstep. He looked up and down the muddy driftway — so correctly named Swale End — before his cottage. His visitor seemed to be alone, and, leaving aside the hour and the as yet unexplained nature of the call, he appeared to be genuine — even to his old fashioned Homburg and the over-conservative cut of his velour overcoat. 'Come in, Mr. Morgan. I'm surprised that you walked down here.'

Morgan removed his hat, and, as Fisher stepped well back into the hall, moved forward and crossed the threshold. 'I had my driver stop on the road,' he explained. 'I would not commit him to, er, unfamiliar ground.'

Despite himself, Fisher laughed at the other's so diplomatic description of the lane that served his property. Then he faced round and said: 'This way.' And after that he led on through into the living room, where he turned again at the room's centre and studied the entering Morgan in the revealing glare of the electric light. Dark-eyed and fiftyish, Morgan had a plump and rather guileless look about him, though his square jaw and well-shaped mouth were firm enough to betray the strength of character behind his air of spruce innocence, and his gaze had a penetrating, quizzical quality which was not at first apparent. 'I was about to have a drink,' Fisher said. 'Will you join me?'

'No, thank you,' Morgan replied, taking a folded card from an inside pocket and opening it so that Fisher could see the photograph it carried, the Home Office franking, Morgan's signature, and that of the Home Secretary beneath it. 'Are you satisfied?'

Fisher nodded. 'I'm convinced,' he said, going to the sideboard and pouring a stiff whisky for himself, where he then stood, the glass untouched in his hand, and smiled ironically as Morgan glanced round the comfortable but very far from luxurious contents of the room while putting his identity card away again. 'Not quite what you expected?'

'Not quite,' Morgan admitted. 'I recognise the need for seclusion, but — you seem to enjoy a measure of success.'

'This is the world of illusion, Mr. Morgan,' Fisher said, very much doubting that the man from the Home Office would exactly understand the religious idiom to which the term applied.

'Nothing,' Morgan agreed significantly, 'is as it seems to be. The true values are all reversed.'

Fisher was indeed surprised. Morgan had known what he was talking about. Perhaps the man was less of the earth-earthy than he appeared. Spirit and a leaning towards self-indulgence could sometimes go together.

Then Morgan surprised him even more. 'We have need of your special knowledge, Mr. Fisher — your unusual character. That's why I'm here.'

'The Home Office?' Fisher queried, for there seemed to have been something more in the man's voice than that.

'All of us,' Morgan answered, his shrug almost one of embarrassment. 'Mankind.'

'It's one thing for the book critics to lay it on thick,' Fisher commented, setting his glass down on the sideboard and gesturing an annoyance which covered the much that he had left unsaid.

'Specifically, then — at this moment — the Government,' Morgan modified.

'That's better,' Fisher said. 'But what can I possibly do for it?'

'Accompany me to R.A.F. Brawdon,' the man from the Home Office replied. 'Stay with me through a flight to a spot on the Yorkshire Moors. And then, dispensing with my company, join person or persons unknown to you in a journey by air to a place unknown to me — and the Government, I must add — somewhere on the world's surface.'

'Are you out of your mind?' Fisher asked quietly. 'Or do you imagine that I am?'

'Neither the one nor the other,' Morgan retorted. 'You asked what you could do for the Government. I have told you.' He raised the white palm of an abruptly staying hand. 'Before you refuse, or show me the door, I must ask you to listen to such explanation of this business as I am able to give.'

'I'm not sure that I want to hear you, Mr. Morgan,' Fisher said, fancying that where the other had been slightly suppliant before there was now a touch of authority creeping in. 'This is Nineteen-eighty-one. I know we've been in the hands of the socialists for a lot of years, but this is still a free country, isn't it?'

'I was not exaggerating when I said that we *all* have need of you,' Morgan replied, dodging the question-mark. 'You could stand between the human race and disaster.'

This got worse. Fisher was tempted to wonder whether his visitor had in fact escaped from a mental home. But, reasonably, there was still no getting away from the man's identity card. 'I don't see myself as a latter-day saviour, Mr. Morgan, and altruism on the scale that you are suggesting strikes me as a mammoth impertinence. Kindly explain yourself in full — or wish me good-night. Frankly, I've had a trying day, and I can do without this addition to it.'

'May I sit down, Mr. Fisher?'

'Please do.' Fisher indicated the worn leather armchairs which stood one on either side of the hearth. They walked to them and sat down, Morgan on the right and his host on the left. It occurred to Fisher that the room was cold, and he switched on the three bars of the electric fire. 'Well?'

'We have an intruder in our midst,' Morgan said. 'He has made contact with the British Government as a prelude to making contact with the United Nations. At this time our intruder is describing himself as a 'benevolent presence', but he has provided plenty of evidence that he is capable of becoming something very different if he wishes.

'In the course of your researches, you must have come upon many cases of mysterious disappearance. I am referring to the kind of disappearance which occurred when five torpedo bombers took off from Fort Lauderdale, Florida, on

December the fifth Nineteen-forty-five, and were never seen again. Then there was the case of the junk that vanished from the heart of a fishing fleet off South Japan, and the no less classic disappearances of the British South American Airways planes Ariel and Star Tiger over the Caribbean. There are many other examples — some earlier than the ones I've mentioned, and some much later — and I've no doubt that you can call a number of them to mind.

'Not to put too fine a point on it, numerous scientific bodies and investigating parties have, across the years, looked into these disappearances as carefully as possible, and their unanimous conclusion has been that you can only account for them if you accept that strange and inexplicable forces must have been in operation. There has been talk of time traps, holes in time, dematerialisation, removal by inter-galactic transmat beams, teleportation, and the Lord only knows what else. As a fairly simple sort of fellow, I have always inclined to the view — in so far as I had ever given it serious thought until just lately — that untraceable accident had played a much larger part in these disappearances than the experts had been prepared to admit, and that if, in a proportion of the cases, some extra-normal agency had been at work, then that agency was of this world and already in some degree recognised and understood by us.

'It seems that I was both right and wrong. The agency is — by recent adoption, at least — of this world, and it has been using a superior technology to analyse our military and productive capabilities, and has now reached the stage at which it is ready to reveal itself and, in pursuit of its initial aims, to demonstrate that its previously hidden activities can be used as a politically coercive argument which the nations of our planet would be mad to ignore. In short, the intruder wants something of us — knows himself in strength — and means to have it.'

'What does he want?' Fisher asked. 'Land? Secrets? Resources? People? What?'

'It hasn't been communicated yet,' Morgan answered. 'You, as our representative — our ambassador, perhaps? — will be told. Her Majesty's Government suspects the obvious — land. An enemy capable of waging war on a technological level on which we could not hope to match him would clearly be prepared to kill millions in order to get his way were it not for doing the planet irreparable ecological harm in the process.'

'How can you be sure that the intruder's capabilities are that great?' Fisher demanded, instinctively incredulous despite his mind's long training to the acceptance of the bizarre and extraordinary. 'How did he get in touch with you? He could be using the mysterious disappearances of the last generation or so as a means of frightening us into the belief that we have an inadequate capacity to fight back. What certainty have you of anything? It could all be an enormous confidence trick.'

Morgan dipped into his inside pocket again. He produced two photographs and handed them to Fisher, who glanced first at one and then the other, a gasp of amazement escaping him, for the pictures were three dimensional to the degree that they created the illusion of space within the room's space, and were plainly so far ahead of even Earth's most advanced photographic techniques that their origin had to be alien. But that was very far from being all of it, since the first of the pictures had for its subject three large aircraft, one bomber and two airliners — all three more than thirty years out of date. The machines were standing on the ground in a cavernous place, and the names Ariel and Star Tiger were visible on the airliners, while the bomber, a Superfortress of the old United States Army Air Force, had the painting of a blonde on its nose that bore the caption 'Honey baby'. The second photograph was still more incredible, for it showed one of the airliners — the Star Tiger — being drawn into the hull of a cigar-shaped spaceship, which looked half as big as a town, by what could only be a tremendous magnetic force, and the single example was enough to explain all

the previously inexplicable disappearances, by air, sea, and land, in the Earth's
records. 'I don't see how they can be
fakes,' Fisher admitted, returning the
photographs to Morgan.

'There are others,' the man from the
Home Office said. 'A dozen or more. I
selected these two because of their
maximum impact. The cases of the
aircraft involved are, of course, particularly well remembered, and the action of
the spaceship is graphic in the extreme. I
have sufficient certainty of the intruder's
power to wish not to fight him, haven't
you — now? Incidentally, the other
photographs hold the faces of people long
supposed to be dead; and Mr. Hento
himself is further proof that all to do with
the 'benevolent presence' is genuine.
While he can pass in one of our crowds, a
man with a skin of a light tan colour,
silvery eyes, and snow white hair is
sufficiently out of the common run for it
to be plain that he belongs to no Earthly
race.'

'Mr. Hento?' Fisher prompted. 'Who
the devil is he?'

'The go-between,' Morgan replied. 'The alien who first made contact with the Home Office. We have learned nothing of day-to-day importance from him about the people he represents. He merely smiled when we asked where he came from in this world — and elsewhere.'

'You must have had him followed!'

'Oh, yes, Mr. Fisher,' Morgan agreed. 'The best men in the Special Branch have tried to shadow him, but he seems to have an unfortunate habit of turning corners and then vanishing.'

'That could be remarkable,' Fisher responded — 'or no more than proof that the Special Branch is not infallible. By what method did this Mr. Hento first get in touch with you?'

'By the least remarkable of all. The photographs were sent to the Home Office through the post. There was a covering letter which suggested that, on the strength of what they revealed, an interview might be in order, and a Bayswater address was given for our reply. I was present when the Home Secretary met him, and Hento made no bones about the fact that he was a kind of interplanetary secret agent — one of a good many who have been moving among us for many years. Then he told the H.S. that the Power he serves is ready to bring to fruition the purpose for which it came to this planet, and that his leader wishes to meet and discuss matters with you and no other.'

'It doesn't make sense!' Fisher protested. 'I've no political gifts; I'm not even interested in politics. I'm not a negotiator of any sort. I've only a passing knowledge of world affairs. I'm a writer on occult matters. Or have been. I had just decided to change my occupation when you knocked on my door. There isn't enough money in writing my kind of books.'

'I had gathered that,' Morgan said shortly. 'But I still don't seem to have got through to you. This goes deeper than your personal needs and prejudices. I mentioned your knowledge and character for the special things they are. Mr. Hento describes you as one of this world's enlightened: a man on the brink of cosmic consciousness; one with a breadth and sympathy that reaches out to life in all its forms and wherever it exists. Mr. Hento sums you up as a 'man for tomorrow'.'

'That's flattering,' Fisher commented — 'if vague. I see myself as a kind of over-aged apprentice to the building supply industry. Mr. Hento would be well advised to look for his spiritualised version of Superman elsewhere. I would be obliged if you'd tell him that.'

'I'm sure I made it plain that a coercive element is present in this.'

'You did,' Fisher agreed rather cynically. 'I was wondering when we would get back to that.'

'*I*', Morgan insisted, 'am not threatening *you*, Mr. Fisher. What threat there is comes from Elsewhere and encompasses all the people of the globe.' He frowned, and made a half-defeated gesture. 'At that, it would be hard to say that Mr. Hento had openly thrown his alien weight around. There was just a reminder. The names of John Greeley, George Turner, and William Ten Bruik were quoted by him, and we were left to hunt down the reference for ourselves. Through our own and the Dutch Police records, we discovered that the three men named were cremated by a, to this day, unexplained process of spontaneous combustion, on the seventh of April, Nineteen-thirty-eight. It is a weird and fascinating story that is too long to go into here, and it might be less ominously relevant had another case of the same kind not occurred at what could well have been the same time as Hento was talking in the Home Office. Before the evening of the day, you see, a report came in from Durham concerning a man who had, during the mid-afternoon, been spontaneously cremated in the privacy of his lavatory. It seems that this fellow had been under the eye of the Police for some time, and was suspected of being a child-murderer. His loss is no tragedy. However, when Mr. Hento wrote to the Home Secretary again, he mentioned the matter — the exact facts of which had been kept out of the newspapers — giving the dead man's name and the exact map co-ordinates for his home; and, as he also asked to see my chief concerning the travel arrangements for the meeting between his leader and you, the Home Secretary was far more disposed to meet him and discuss the matter than might have been the case.'

'The implications would seem to be rather obvious,' Fisher admitted.

Morgan nodded emphatically. 'Setting aside the chance that a far-seeing justice has so far been behind these forces of remote combustion, no man, woman, or child is safe from them ultimately.'

'The pressures to enforce my co-operation are there,' Fisher said heavily. 'I see the thread of credibility, but it's the lack of plausibility that worries me. I have the feeling that somewhere in all this I'm being had for a fool, and I'm not going to be made a fool of by anybody.'

Then, at Fisher's back, there was a kind of muffled explosion, and it was followed by roaring sounds, heat, and a smell of burning varnish. Fisher craned and saw his desk blazing merrily; but, though the warning in what had occurred hit him in the same instant of awareness, he kept his head and left his chair in a fast but orderly manner, rounding the already erect Morgan's seat and passing through the door near the inner left-hand corner of the room to enter the kitchen, where, knowing the age and tinder-dry condition of the property in which he lived, he had always kept a fire extinguisher. Now he snatched down the extinguisher from the clips in which it hung beside the back door and carried it into the living room, pressing its plunger as he approached his burning desk and directing a stream of foam on to the flames. The fire began to die almost at once, and within ten seconds the last of the blaze had been blotted out, leaving behind soot, fumes, and generally sticky mess — not to mention curtains that hung in black rags, a ruined mat, and areas of wallpaper nearby that had been scorched out of recognition. It went without saying, of course, that the desk itself had been damaged beyond all fitness for further use, and it appeared probable that its contents had also ceased to have any practical value. So much for those written pages of *Inhabitants of Time*, and a stack of notes comprising weeks of research and at least forty thousand words of holograph.

'I think a point has been made,' Morgan said from the back of the room.

'Driven home would be more correct,' Fisher replied, setting his fire extinguisher down on the hearth.

'You know what acquiesence with the inevitable equates,' Morgan went on significantly. 'I would like you to come with me straightaway, Mr. Fisher. I understand that every provision is to be made for your comfort. Wherever you are going, you will be treated as an honoured guest.'

Again passing his gaze over the fire damage, Fisher smiled ironically at that one; but then he turned to Morgan and nodded. 'What's the sense in hanging about? If you'll go out first, Mr. Morgan, I'll put my jacket on and lock up behind us.'

'Thank you,' Morgan returned, his too quick smile betraying the load which had just been lifted from his mind.

Fisher watched the man leave the room. Then he listened to his footsteps as he walked down the hall and passed out through the front door. It was hard to credit that Morgan was real, and almost impossible to accept the alien imperative of which his words had been the harbinger. In cliché terms, it had all been so sudden. The sense of life's straight line had been irretrievably broken; the future had suddenly gone off at a tangent from the present. He was afraid; there was in him a creeping prescience that chilled his spine and made him want to jump through the window and make a run for it. He had touched the fringes of something that was not good. There was no benevolence in a Power that enjoined secrecy and made force its example. Yet he knew that he must go to meet whatever lay ahead. Even if he were prepared to gamble with his own life, he could not take the smallest risk that might endanger others. The touch of destiny could never be mistaken. There was no escape.

He took down his jacket from the back

of the door and pulled it on; then, as he was he was taking a last, disapproving look round and preparing to step out into the hall, he saw the glass of whisky that he had earlier poured for himself still standing on the sideboard. Reaching out, he picked the drink up and raised it to his lips. He might as well get it down. There was no telling when he would get the next one.

2

For the last three minutes tall, dense
thorn hedges had stood between the two
men and the sky. Now Fisher and
Morgan had almost reached the end of
their walk from the cottage to the main
road. They had just put the last of the
corners in the lane's snaking course
behind them, and Fisher could see the
tarmac ramp at the end of the way which
formed the link between the rutted link
track and the A class highway which it
served. Water lay upon the tilted bitumen,
its presence reflecting the moonlight, and
beyond it, set back from the slight ascent,
was a glimpse of the hedge at the further
side of the main road and the big car
that was standing on the grass verge
before it.

'Your car?' Fisher asked conversationally.

'Yes,' Morgan answered. 'And no.
Properly speaking, it is a staff car and
belongs to the Home Office.'

Fisher nodded. A staff car, perhaps; but one obviously used by only the most senior of staff. It was a Rolls Royce, and, as he and Morgan finished climbing the ramp and prepared to step out on to the main road, Fisher made out the straight-backed silhouette of the uniformed man who was sitting in the driver's seat. He didn't wonder that Morgan had told the chauffeur not to leave the highway. It would indeed have been a form of sacrilege to have exposed such a mechanical aristocrat to the flints and potholes of the lane; but it also said much for Morgan's humility that he had been prepared to take to his feet and walk down to Swale End. The man was plainly something more than one of your average Civil Service stuffed shirts. But that, of course, had been fairly apparent from the start.

They began crossing the road. The chauffeur looked round at their approach. He hastily stubbed out a cigarette, and began to open the door beside him, but Morgan waved at him negatively and said: 'Stay where you are, Britling.'

The chauffeur gave his head a jerk.

Morgan opened the car's rear off-side door. 'In you get, Mr. Fisher.'

Fisher got in. The leather upholstery of the back seat yielded under his rump, but it was cold, and he gave a shiver. Late October was time for a topcoat. He ought to have brought one along.

Morgan flopped down at Fisher's side, then pulled the door shut after him. 'R.A.F. Brawdon,' he said in answer to the question that Britling's pale, thin face craned at him.

'Yes, sir,' the chauffeur replied, his cockney accent noticeable. 'Have to turn round up the road somewhere.'

'Do the best you can,' Morgan acknowledged.

Britling switched on the headlamps and started up. The car left the grass verge with hardly a murmur or a lurch. Its lights beamed whitely into the cloud-blackened gloom of the land to windward, then swung back to pick out the road ahead as an almost perfect strip of cobbler's wax and liquorice.

Fisher said: 'A side road opens on the

left and not more than a quarter of a mile away. Britling can turn there.'

'Did you hear that, Britling?' Morgan asked.

'Yes, sir. I believe I can see the junction now.'

'It's an out-of-the-way spot I live in,' Fisher went on. 'Did you have much difficulty finding it, Mr. Morgan?'

'Rather!' the man from the Home Office confirmed. 'A chap on a bicycle finally put us right.'

'A writer needs peace and quiet. I bought Swale End some years ago, to give me just that and to discourage visitors. One of the unhappy facts about working at home is that friends and relations see you as a retired man, and behave accordingly.'

'I can imagine.'

Fisher privately doubted it. People seldom could. Work carried out at home was always supposed to get done by a magic that was not apparent elsewhere. But Morgan clearly did not want to hear about it, so he said no more.

The Rolls came to the side road. As

might have been expected, it was in the hands of a first class driver and made the neatest of neat turns. After that it sped back in the direction from which it had come, passed the head of the lane from which Fisher and Morgan had so recently emerged, and approached the lights of Cleggburgh, the small Lincolnshire town in which the former had been born behind his father's tailor-and-outfitter's shop and lived out his school and formative years, returning after university to serve for a period in the archives of the local newspaper and then betake himself to Swale End and the literary life, a break with the safety of an assured income which had infuriated his father and lost him the better part of his expectations to a number of charitable institutions when the old man had died.

Its speed greatly reduced, the Rolls entered Cleggburgh's high street. Fisher gave an eye to the familiar shops, the pubs, the bingo hall, the school, the supermarket and the service station, then watched Tommy Stark's warehouse and yard slide by, asking himself whether this strange affair in which he had become so reluctantly involved would turn out after all to be a variety of damp squib and find him in Tommy's office on the Monday of next week. His forebodings had relaxed against the soothing influences of moon-light and movement, and he hoped it would turn out to be so. It was a truism that the worst worries were usually the ones that never happened.

They cleared the town. Flat land showed ahead and on the left, while on the right the moon picked out the black mudflats and oily waters of the Wash. Fisher was glad that the windows of the car were shut and the smell of Britling's cigarette lingered, for he had never been able to stand the heavy, rotten odour of the — as he regarded it — open sewer in which King John was said to have lost his treasure.

The car kept up its almost soundless progress for another four or five miles. Then a crossroads appeared ahead. Here the chauffeur slowed down and peered closely through the windscreen, turning off to the left as his lights shone on the

R.A.F. Brawdon sign. After that the vehicle headed down a narrowing road for about a mile, and then the runway lights and control tower beacons of the aerodrome came into view on the right, and before long the chauffeur turned into a posted entrance on that side and came to a halt before the whitened barrier outside the guard-room.

The guard commander came out at once. Morgan's business had obviously travelled ahead of him, and the airman checked the Rolls and its occupants on to the premises with a minimum of delay. Then the man pointed out the Headquarters building, a large, square, well-lighted structure which stood beyond a street or two of married quarters, and Britling moved on again, following the white-washed kerbstones of the drome's main avenue on a right-hand curve through the residential area and out to another stop in front of the H.Q., where a short, slimly built, immaculate-looking officer, who wore gold braid on his hat and had a too severe expression on his sharply incised, disciplinarian's features, was waiting for them at the top of the steps that led up to the building's front door. The officer had a man in flying kit on either side of him, and, as Britling got out of the Rolls and opened the door at Morgan's side, the three of them began marching down the steps.

Morgan left the car, and Fisher stepped to the ground behind him. 'I'm Morgan,' the man from the Home Office said, as the trio of R.A.F. men reached the bottom of the steps and the officer with the gold braid on his hat snapped off the smartest of salutes. 'Group Captain Maynard?'

'Yes, sir.' The pair shook hands. Then the group captain pointed first to his right and then his left. 'May I introduce Flight Lieutenant Saunders and Pilot Officer Mackay? They will fly you up to the Yorkshire Moors, sir.'

'Gentlemen,' Morgan acknowledged, shaking hands with them also, then nodding at Fisher. 'This is our V.I.P. He shall go nameless for tonight. We shall set him down at the given map reference, and after that we shall forget what he looks like and any unusual happenings in which he may be concerned. Is that understood?'

'Perfectly, sir,' Flight Lieutenant Saunders answered, a dark eye just missing Fisher as it slanted speculatively in his rakish jib.

'They have been thoroughly briefed on the strict secrecy of this mission, sir,' the group captain assured Morgan.

'Good,' the man from the Home Office said briskly. 'Let's get on with it, shall we?'

Maynard raised a hand and beckoned peremptorily towards a station waggon that was standing at the corner of the H.Q. building on his left. The vehicle revved into motion, its lights flashing on, passed down the near-side of the Rolls Royce, and halted a short distance ahead of it. 'If you and your V.I.P. will get in, Mr. Morgan,' Maynard said, gesturing towards the newly arrived car, 'my officers will join you, and then the driver will take you all out to the helicopter pad.'

'Thank you, Group Captain,' Morgan replied, as the R.A.F. driver walked round his vehicle and opened the doors for his expected passengers. 'I hope I haven't spoiled your night.'

'It's a commanding officer's business to be on duty when he's needed, sir,' Maynard answered. 'I hope you'll do me the honour of joining me for a drink when you get back.'

'I'd be delighted,' Morgan said, craning out of the lead that he had already started giving towards the station waggon.

They reached the vehicle. Morgan got into it and sat down on its back seat, where Fisher joined him, and then the two officers in flying kit entered also and sat down on the car's middle seat, which was situated in front of the civilians. After that the driver shut the doors and took his seat behind the wheel, letting in his clutch at a sign from his commanding officer and then heading into the darkness that existed to the north of the largest of the aerodrome's lighted areas.

The station waggon's headlights entered and followed the slow bend of the perimeter track. Fisher saw drizzle gather on the windscreen, and watched the wiper brush it off again. A match flared as Flight Lieutenant Saunders lighted a cigarette, and the flame showed up a number of details on the map which the boyish-looking Pilot Officer Mackay was holding in his left hand. The flight lieutenant glanced round, but didn't speak, and then he looked to the front again, smoke pouring out of his nostrils as he extinguished his match with a shake. Then the driver changed down, turned left into a dispersal area, swung right a moment later, and drew to a halt with his headlamps shining into the open hatch in the side of a big helicopter. Now Saunders said: 'Well, here we are.' And he opened the door beside him and slipped quickly out of the car, accepting a salute as two men in forage caps and mechanics' overalls appeared from the gloom on the left. After that, as Mackay joined him outside, he reached for the middle seat and pulled it forward, thus giving the two men in the rear of the vehicle free passage to the tarmac on which he stood. 'If you gentlemen will climb into the helicopter's cabin, Mackay and I will see about getting us into the air.

Fisher followed Morgan out of the station waggon. They crossed the ground which lay between them and the helicopter. Then they stepped up into the body of the machine, which was shuddering slightly in the motion of its feathered vanes, and turned to look out of the hatch. Fisher watched Mackay climb into the helicopter through the forward door that gave access to the flight deck, then saw the flight lieutenant sign a sheet by the light of the taller mechanic's torch, acknowledge a further salute, and finally swing up into the machine by the same route which the pilot officer had used.

A few moments later, Mackay appeared in the cabin. He turned on a rather dim light, shut the sliding door through which the two civilians had been looking out, and pointed to the seat that ran along the opposite wall. 'Make yourselves as comfortable as you can,' he advised. 'Sorry we're not fixed up for luxury flying. We normally do air-sea rescue duties.'

'We're only interested in utility,' Morgan replied. 'You can land almost anywhere.

That's what is so important to us.'

'There's a lot to be said for the old chopper,' Mackay agreed, turning away and walking back to the flight deck, where he sat down in the navigator's chair and spread his map on the table before him, nodding to the man in the pilot's seat adjacent that all was well.

Saunders spoke to the control tower. He was given permission to take off. Increasing power, he lifted the machine into the air and sped off to the right, climbing fast. After that he informed his controller that he was airborne and on course.

Conscious of the rushing depths under the seat of his trousers, Fisher folded his arms; then, twisting slightly from the waist, he gazed out into the northern sky through the perspex screens of the flight deck. The night was thin on stars and disfigured by enormous blotches of inky cloud. And the higher the helicopter rose, the harder the wind kicked it; and presently rain splattered blobs and rivulets of obscurity on the screens and silhouetted Saunders and Mackay against them with a sharpness of line which had not been present before. There was interest in the sight, but it soon passed, and Fisher found boredom creeping into him as the minutes slowly succeeded one another. 'I'm beginning to feel like a character from a spy story,' he announced in a moment of sour humour. 'I take it the secrecy is to keep the newshounds out of your hair.'

'Yes,' Morgan replied. 'We can do without the kind of complications which might arise from panicking a worldwide search for the hiding place of the aliens.'

'What will their secret be worth once I have been in and out of it?'

'We have to trust their judgement,' Morgan commented. 'Perhaps it won't matter then. Possibly I have led you to presume too much. Hospitality can include a blindfold.'

'So can a great many other things,' Fisher reflected. 'If you have led me to presume too much, there can be only one sufferer.'

'That unfortunately is true. I would help it if I could, but it isn't within my power to do so. Your safety lies in your importance to the aliens. But a good deal must also depend on you. The Government does not require you to play the hero. Don't be too curious — do only what's asked of you. Be polite and accommodating. At least seem to respect the other man and his point of view.'

'Be a diplomat.'

'Exactly.'

'Why Craig Fisher?'

'Why Herod? Why Karl Marx? Why — Christ?'

Fisher blew out his cheeks, and shook his head. The argument was essentially as old as the human race. He knew that he could no more supply an answer to it than could the luckless of a thousand generations before him. The problem was his. Perhaps, in accord with his persuasion towards predestination and heavenly computers, he had devised the test for himself. If that were so, he had no cause to complain — must complain no further. But faith, as between a man and his typewriter, was a very different thing from faith in the purpose of those manifestations in his life which he preferred to regard as peradventure and outside any part of his own design.

Wishing to be certain that he could find no special inspiration, Fisher concentrated on the subject for a minute or two longer, but then it began to seem too tenuous and unhelpful to bother with, and he returned to his contemplation of the sky beyond the flight deck. He relaxed; the engines throbbed hypnotically, and the rotors spread their repressive vibrations through the craft and the air about it's fuselage; sleep trembled a response in his eyelids. But then Pilot Officer Mackay reappeared in the cabin, and he held in his hands a half-gallon thermos flask and a couple of plastic cups. 'Coffee?' he asked.

Both Fisher and Morgan answered in the affirmative.

Mackay passed the plastic cups to the men before him. Then he uncorked the flask and poured for them, a strong smell of whisky rising with the steam from the hot coffee. 'We've just passed over the

Humber, gentlemen. About half way. Okay?'

The seated pair nodded enthusiastically between sips.

Mackay remained by them long enough to top up their cups. Then he replaced the cork in his flask and returned to the front of the helicopter. Resuming his seat on the flight deck, he exchanged a few words with the pilot, then gave himself up to quartering the sky ahead, the thermos resting in his lap as a warmer for his fingers.

Time went by; and, judging by what Mackay had said about the half-way mark, Fisher decided that the flight must have entered its final stages. He felt a churning in his stomach, and a tightness developed in his chest. The unknown was near at hand; reality was thrusting hard. He caught himself in a sidelong glance of dislike at Morgan, which he knew to be unjustified. Then the helicopter began to lose altitude, and not long after that — confirming the accuracy of his subconscious calculations — the machine touched down with a small bump and there was an immediate reduction of noise and vibration as the pilot feathered the rotors and called back: 'We've arrived, as per flight plan! Nothing in sight — if you discount a lot of rural Yorkshire!'

'Thank you,' Morgan replied, rising to his feet and sliding open the hatch in the wall opposite him. 'Our V.I.P. and I will get out. You two stay inside.'

'Frank and I will have our coffee now,' the pilot agreed indifferently, looking to the front again.

Morgan jumped heavily to the ground below him, and Fisher dropped out stiffly in the man's wake. They walked away from the helicopter, and stopped on open grass about a hundred and fifty yards beyond it. The wind ruffled at them coldly, and blustered through the pasture at their feet; but weather conditions up here were a big improvement on those which they had left in Lincolnshire. The night was clear to the horizons, and the glow of the waxing moon was unobstructed. Clutching his jacket about him, Fisher gazed through the vaults of shining emptiness and detected the shadows of a small grandeur to the north of them. 'The Cleveland Hills,' Morgan said, following his companion's eye. 'The Vale of Pickering lies rather less than ten miles to our right. Our elevation is about seven hundred feet, and our position is about as remote from the masses of humanity as it is possible to get in this England of ours.'

'I understood we were to be met,' Fisher said.

'We were given the date of the rendezvous, its position, and the approximate hour,' Morgan answered defensively.

'Which is?'

'Oh two hundred.'

'What's the time now?'

Morgan turned up his left wrist and peered closely at the face of his watch. 'Oh one fifty.'

'We're early,' Fisher said dryly. 'I was hoping the other party might have been and gone.'

'I suspect he was watching our arrival,' Morgan returned, tilting his head sharply backwards as a shrill whistling noise came out of the sky above them and a large circular shape sliced through the air

46

directly over their heads and seemed about to slam into the ground nearby, only to check into a hover at the last instant and then settle to earth with a touch so gentle that it added a hundred-fold to the spectacular effect of its approach.

'Here,' Fisher remarked, trying to deny the tremble which had entered his hands, 'the question so long in debate is answered. Flying saucers are a material reality.'

'This one certainly is,' Morgan agreed as lights blazed up under the cupola of the disc-shaped flying machine before them, figures became visible at its machinery and control panels, and a hold opened in its side and an articulated stairway came thrusting into view under the guidance of a robot regulator. 'So is the man coming out of it.'

Now Fisher also detected the figure of the man who had appeared in the darkness at the top of the steps. He watched the other's progress down the stair and then across the grass towards him and Morgan. The alien's shape took

47

on detail as he drew nearer, and it became apparent that he was of no more than average size, and wore clothing that was Earth-type in every respect. His garments consisted of a trench-coat, drainpipes, highly polished shoes with pointed toes, and a Tyrolean hat that sported a feather in its band. He carried an umbrella in his right hand, and, if his appearance in the light from the saucer was a little showy, it was also immaculate.

'Good morning,' the alien minced out, his English seemingly as perfect as the rest of him.

'Mr. Hento,' Morgan said in evident surprise.

'Indeed, Mr. Morgan,' the other agreed. 'You did not expect to see me? Tut, tut. But how could you? I had not been told that I was to be in charge of this part of the operation when last we met, so I could not say anything to prepare you.'

'Well met anyway,' the man from the Home Office said in a rather forced voice. 'This is Craig Fisher.'

Hento removed his hat, held it against

his chest, and bowed to Fisher. 'Your servant, sir. I trust the, er, fire in your home did only minimal damage?'

'I imagine that's no thanks to you,' Fisher retorted, incensed by a faintly mocking note in the alien's theatrical urbanity.

'You took the point,' Hento reminded.

'Men with such intrusive ways about them are unlikely to endear themselves to the people of this world, Mr. Hento,' Fisher observed. 'Among the first of the lessons we teach our children is that of respecting the privacy of others.'

'You have no monopoly of good manners, sir,' Hento protested. 'We make no habit of looking into private places. On the other hand, our current situation occasionally forces us into actions that we, in our higher selves, regret. Your desk was such a case. But it is as well that you should know the extent of our power before we start.'

'Start what?'

'I am merely an underling, Mr. Fisher,' Hento said. 'Is it kind to ask an underling questions that he has been given no permission to answer?'

Fisher raised an eyebrow. While keeping him guessing, Hento had also justified himself and deftly returned the lesson in manners of a minute ago. There was nothing elfin or extra-normal about Mr. Hento; he possessed a craft, sensitivity, and incipient malice that were wholly human; and the machine behind him was a further and convincing proof of the advanced nature of the Power which employed him. It was all for real, as the Americans were wont to say. Fisher's last flicker of hope vanished. He was not the victim of a bizarre charade. There was to be no eleventh hour let off. He must pull himself together: take Morgan's advice and start playing the diplomat. So very much more than just his safety could depend on his bringing out the best in himself. 'Whatever your occupational status, Mr. Hento,' he said, 'I am at your command.'

'There speaks the true man!' Hento declared. 'You are at the beginning of a task which will give your life an added worth. The journeys between my people and yours will soon become a common-place for you. Follow me, please.'

'One moment,' Morgan put in. 'When can we expect him back?'

'I cannot say,' Hento replied. 'It does not rest with me.'

'Where will the return be made?'

Hento shook his head. 'I will be in touch.'

Morgan gestured his inability to do or say more.

'It's all right,' Fisher said. 'Au revoir.'

'Au revoir. And — good luck.'

'Thanks.' Fisher moved in pursuit of the retreating Hento, but was still several paces behind when the alien reached the disc-shaped flying machine. He expected Hento to turn and wait for him at the foot of the steps which led into the craft, but the other went straight up the stair and passed from sight. Fisher realized then that Hento was trying to demonstrate perfect trust in him, and he responded by trotting up the steps and entering the warm, pleasant-smelling interior of the saucer's control room as if he felt no uneasiness at all.

There were three men seated at the control consoles. They were clad in tight-fitting uniforms. These comprised jackets and trousers that were white down the right-hand side and black down the left. They also wore plastic boots which matched the colour scheme and a type of black and white forage cap. As with Hento — who had taken a wall seat on the further side of the round chamber and sat in smiling placidity with the point of his unbrella resting between his feet and his hands pressing down on its handle — they tended to an aquilinity of feature and had skin that was slightly darkened, while their eyes had a silvery, almost dead appearance and the hair that was visible around the sides of their heads was as white as the driven snow. But, if the crewmen were openly curious where he was concerned, they were also friendly, and smiled when he smiled, and one of them — the captain, presumably, judging from the three vertical red bars on the breastpocket of his coat — made a polite signal for him to sit down on a wall seat that balanced the position in which

Hento sat; and, as he seated himself, a lever was pressed and the steps outside the saucer's exit folded back into their hold, while the door itself slid shut and totally separated the interior of the cupola from the night without. After that the main lights were extinguished, leaving only the glow of the consoles to light the crew to their work; and then another lever was thrust forward and the power unit began to pulse and hum, and a moment later the machine seemed to spring into the air and started moving upwards at a speed that was almost unbelievable. Screwing his head round, Fisher looked out and down through the transparency of the cupola. For an instant the R.A.F. helicopter was visible; then it and the ground were totally lost to view and the alien craft rushed higher and higher up the tunnel of the night. Then, as it seemed that it must rocket onwards until it ended among the stars, it shifted in a split second from vertical to oblique flight and rode a path of moonbeams on a still narrowly climbing course to the north. 'An admirable form of transport, don't you think?' Mr. Hento asked across the murmur of the control room's propulsive energies.

'Excellent,' Fisher agreed.

'First class for stratospheric flight,' Hento went on, 'though too small and slow for true space flight.'

'Slow?' Fisher wondered.

'How do you measure fifteen thousand miles per hour against a single light year?'

'That sum is quite beyond me,' Fisher admitted. 'Where do you come from' — he gestured towards infinity — 'out there?'

Hento smiled his beatific smile, but made no reply.

'Mars? Venus?'

The smile became more sharply defined, and for a second or two it seemed that Hento still would not speak; but all at once he said: 'I think I may safely say further than that. Oh, much further than that.'

'Where are we going now?'

'Soon, sir, you will be among those only too willing to answer your questions.'

'Even at this stage it remains a secret?'

'No. We are going to a place that is situated well above latitude sixty six and a half degrees north.'

'Into the Arctic Circle!'

'Towards the upper end of Greenland in fact.'

'But there's nothing there!' Fisher protested. 'Just ice and snow, and it's almost too cold for human beings to exist!'

'There is a lot of ice and snow there,' Hento agreed, 'and I believe it is very cold.'

'You believe,' Fisher murmured incredulously. 'I haven't experienced the cold,' Hento explained blandly.

'I was right to take it that your people live up there?'

'That is what I wished to convey.'

'Are you, then, so different from us? Can you stand extremes of temperature that would — '

'By no means,' Hento interrupted. 'Of the two peoples, we are the less able to stand climatic extremes.'

'I have a suspicion you're mocking me, Mr. Hento.'

'Not at all, sir,' Hento assured him. 'But if it pleases you to imagine otherwise — We are now passing over the North Atlantic and approaching Iceland. We should reach journey's end a few minutes from now.'

Fisher felt more than ever baffled by the mystery of it all. He experienced an irritating desire to go on questioning Hento, but the questions that he could ask seemed to have exhausted themselves. Sitting back, he let silence reassert itself and tried to imagine the kind of 'as the crow flies' travel that could reduce a journey of more than two thousand miles to something less in terms of time than the run between Ongar and the Bank on the London underground. Speeds far in excess of fifteen thousand miles per hour had been reached by Earth's rocketry — escape velocity was in the region of twenty six thousand miles per hour — but such speeds were attained by vast and clumsy vehicles under conditions of extreme boost. Here there was a fairy lightness about the whole process: no thunderous accelerations, no crushing eruptions of gas, no do-or-burst rigidity that was always on the edge of dissolution. There was at present little sense of movement at all, and yet the saucer had already whirled its way across a large piece of the northern hemisphere. Even Concorde was still far removed from the true stratospheric flight being demonstrated here.

Presently the man whom Fisher had taken to be the captain made a small adjustment to the controls. The line of flight began to decline. Soon the dim emptiness of the upper atmosphere started to lose its backdrop of glittering stars and vapours washed around the saucer's cupola and clung. There were signs of ice that even the alien defrosting devices could not dispel. Agitation became apparent around the machine; winds began to buffet. Then white lightning ripped the gloom, and thunder rolled like cries of terror trapped in the deepest cave. After that ice fragments slashed and raked at the saucer out of an Arctic hurricane, and the very existence of the machine seemed to be threatened by forces outside the power of any Science to control.

Fisher set his teeth and tried to remain as unperturbed as his companions seemed to be; and then the pounding abruptly diminished and soon ceased altogether; and after that the saucer spun on through an area of perfect calm — the traces of frost dissolving from its glazed top — and gradually it settled towards a landing, this coming about a minute later and with the same lightness that had been displayed on the Yorkshire Moors.

The lights came on. Then the door was opened, and the articulated stair unfolded beneath it. Hento walked briskly across the floor of the craft and stepped out into the night. Fisher left his seat and moved to the exit. He was prepared to be reduced to a mindless jelly by the hyperborean chill that he expected to meet him. Instead the mildest of air currents played on his features as he passed through the doorway, and he felt the kind of fresh tingling in his blood which he had always associated with spring. Then he walked down the steps in

Hento's wake, aware at once of lights burning nearby on the left and three men clad in white trousers and knee-length, belted robes of the same colour standing on the ground below, their faces turned up into the clear radiance which the saucer's control room was shedding.

Fisher reached the ground. He looked on as Hento bowed deeply to the tallest and most commanding member of the waiting trio and spoke a number of words in a language which he, Fisher, found totally incomprehensible. And when Hento had finished, the tall man nodded, and, inclining his head to Fisher in a way that expressed respect without servility, said in flawless English: 'I am he called Arle. I bid you welcome to New Lexia, Mr. Fisher.'

'Thank you,' Fisher returned; for he didn't see what else he could say.

3

As Fisher's eyes adjusted to the dim scene about him, he became aware of the full wonder of the situation in which he now found himself. It was apparent that the lights on the left belonged to a very large building indeed, and that there were other and less brilliantly illuminated structures beyond and around it. He could also make out the silhouettes of bushes and trees, hear the splash of fountains, and smell the scent of flowers. Yet only a minute or two ago he had been in a flying machine which had been shuddering before the blast of an Arctic storm of the utmost severity. It was like being a waking part of an experience that could only happen in a dream. 'It's almost too much to believe,' he murmured.

'There is a natural explanation for everything,' Arle said in quick understanding. 'This is merely a sanctuary wrested from your frozen North by the mechanical forces of which we Lexians are the masters. Be certain that, within a few miles in any direction of us, the storm still rages.'

'So I am in Greenland.'

'Yes, Mr. Fisher. Not to place your position too exactly, you are standing somewhere between the routes traced by Rasmussen's crossing in Nineteen-twelve and Captain Koch's in Nineteen-thirteen.' Arle chuckled, his features aged and fragile in the fall of light from the saucer. 'The details? Our good Mr. Hento — and others like him — have opened for us all those histories and records which are open to you. You must have realized that we also have scanners that are capable of bringing to us exactly what is happening anywhere on this world at any given moment. Forgive me if I repeat myself. There is *nothing* here that does not have a natural explanation.'

'How long have you been here?' Fisher demanded.

'Forty eight years.'

'Since Nineteen-thirty-three,' Fisher breathed. 'Even longer than I had imagined. Perhaps longer than Mr. Morgan supposes.'

'The life spans of Lexian and Earthman are very similar,' Arle remarked, 'and I was a young man when I was entrusted with the New Lexian Project. There are few of my original team left now. Yes, I see from your face that you are wondering why we have waited so long to make contact with the people of this planet. In the first place we had to work hard to establish ourselves, in the second a global war intervened, and in the third — the inner purpose of our task not having to run to even an approximate deadline until recently — we have been awaiting a time of universal concord and unity. Now, as I have hinted, we are being forced to somewhat premature action; but I will come to that when we go fully into the reason for your being here.'

'When is that to be?' Fisher asked.

'After you have slept for preference. Shortly, if you insist.'

'I insist on nothing, sir.'

'That makes it easier for everybody,' Arle acknowledged. 'I will have a meal brought to you in the dining hall, and then I will show you to the room which you will occupy while you are with us. But first I must introduce my two colleagues.' He turned to the balding, round-bodied man who stood on his right. 'This is Khaka. He is my Deputy Project Chief.' Then he turned to the stoop-shouldered, thin-haired, crafty-looking individual who stood leering on his left. 'This is Doctor Samerle. He is my Scientific Director. These two men are my friends and advisors, and they invariably have a say in the decisions I reach. You will see a good deal of them during your visit.'

Fisher inclined his head. 'Gentlemen.'

Khaka and Samerle tucked their hands into the sleeves of their robes and bent slightly from their waists, their appearance faintly monkish.

'Say farewell to Mr. Fisher, Hento,' Arle advised. 'We are about to take him into Project House.'

'Bye-bye, Mr. Fisher,' Hento said, giving the Earthman a pat on the arm and then stepping on to the stair that gave access to the flying saucer's interior and beginning to climb. 'Must be on my travels. We shall meet again.'

Fisher waved in reply. Then Hento passed into the disc-shaped flying machine, the stairway retracted, the door secured at his back, the control room lights went out, and, as the four watchers outside backed off to a safer distance, the saucer rose into the air and then slanted into a climb southwards, vanishing where the hard clarity of the night sky smudged off into a dark and impermeable haze. 'The books that have been written on the subject of those machines,' Fisher said, shaking his head over a mystery whose explanation seemed disappointing. 'The New Lexian taxi service.'

'Apt,' Arle agreed, his laugh betraying a ready sense of humour as he set off for the huge and brightly lighted building on the left. 'Hento has an appointment in Knightsbridge.'

'One more question for now,' Fisher said, tacking on behind Khaka and Doctor Samerle.

'What is it?' Arle asked without looking round.

'How have you managed to remain undiscovered for the better part of half a century? It occurs to me that Russian aircraft often fly this way, and that the United States airbase of Thule isn't too far off. This place ought to be detectable, in radar terms, for its aerial comings and goings.'

'Who seeks the eye of the hurricane?' Arle inquired. 'Greenland is very large — a land mass of seven hundred and thirty six thousand square miles — and this far north it is frequently ravaged by magnetic storms that make a mockery of radar. Man's disinclination to explore in regions of extreme inclemency has really been our best ally. It was planned that it should be so before our New Lexia Expedition landed here.'

It sounded reasonably convincing, though Fisher was not entirely persuaded. Obviously, if any aircraft or expedition should approach too closely, there was always the spontaneous combustion weapon with which to destroy them. It was all too easy to forget that the pleasant and well-spoken Arle had already notched up many a crime against the people of the Earth. And there was no telling what the snows around New Lexia might hold of the remains of the would-be escapers from among the crews of the aircraft and suchlike that must have been brought here after being seized by the great spaceship seen in the photograph that Morgan had shown him.

They reached the building that Fisher presumed to be Project House. Further light beamed out to meet them as Arle opened the twin leaves of the front door. Then, Khaka holding back to close up behind them, they passed into the hall beyond and strode towards its further end, Fisher noting that the place was heavily buttressed and about as eternal as precise architecture and undressed blocks of granite could make it.

The hall gave into a quarter of closed rooms and criss-cross corridors. Here, at one of the intersections, they came to a railed stairway which descended through the floor. Arle led them downwards into what Fisher regarded as an over-deep basement, and then they moved into a well-lighted but nevertheless grimly austere system of passages which had been cut into the bedrock of the area — which was of the same granite as that used in the building above — and suggested the galleries of a fortress rather than any kind of living place; and it was this notion that brought Fisher to the conclusion that the forethought which seemed to have gone into so much else in New Lexia had here decreed that the lower housing for the Project's staff should be so constructed that it could double as a shelter against aerial attack if the district should come under siege. Not that he thought there was anything very remarkable in his observation. The Lexians were clearly a provident and practical race, and their sheer efficiency would make them formidable opposition in peace or war.

Soon the passages grew larger and less numerous, but Fisher was by now unsure that he could find his way back to the stairway from which the basement began.

Then, in the midst of so much that was confusing and cheerless, they came to a hall which was hung with the most splendid tapestries and lighted by a line of electric chandeliers. At the middle of the hall stood a long refectory table, and around this about forty hoop-backed chairs were positioned; and, as they walked down the arched space, Fisher felt heaters under the floor giving out a gentle warmth, and he saw sideboards and serving trolleys. He saw, too, on the left-hand side of the table's head, a raised panel with a button set in it, and he watched Arle go straight to this button and press it. After that the Lexian Project Chief glanced round and said: 'Please sit down wherever you like, Mr. Fisher. I hope you will not mind eating alone. Had you arrived earlier, you could have dined in the company of New Lexia's most senior people — the administrators and scientists — but it was obviously not possible to be that precise in the arrangements. Our apologies for any deficiencies in our immediate hospitality. I trust you will blame them on circumstances and not your hosts.'

'There's no need for apologies,' Fisher answered, drawing out the chair nearest to him and sitting down rather reluctantly. 'I'm not particularly hungry.'

'Nevertheless,' he was informed, 'you should eat.' And then a man dressed in one of the half black and half white uniforms which he had first seen worn by the crewmen of the flying saucer entered the hall through a door at its upper end and stood to attention near the head of the table while Arle gave him an order in his own tongue. After that the man dipped his head and went out again.

Then Arle turned to Khaka and Doctor Samerle and again spoke words that Fisher didn't understand; and the pair backed off from the craning Earthman, bowed, wished him 'good-night' in English, and withdrew through the door by which the uniformed man had so recently gone out.

Arle sat down in the chair at the top of the table. He gazed before him in a thoughtful, finger-tapping silence that

Fisher judged it better not to break. Then the man dressed in the black and white uniform reappeared. He carried at his chest a large silver tray. On it was a grilled salmon, a joint of meat, three dishes of vegetables, a bowl containing fruits the like of which Fisher had never seen before, and a flagon of wine. The man placed the tray within Fisher's reach, set a plate, goblet, and cutlery in front of him, and then served him with a portion of the salmon and poured wine from the flagon into the goblet. 'Perhaps you will see to yourself in whatever else you need,' Arle said, dismissing the uniformed servant with a peremptory flick of his right hand.

Fisher forked at the thick flesh of the salmon and his taste buds were tickled by the subtle blend of spices which had been used in the fish's preparation. 'You must enjoy good fishing,' he remarked somewhat leadingly.

'We have our waters,' Arle replied.

Smiling, Fisher finished his first portion of the fish and then helped himself to a second; but after that he avoided the meat and vegetables and went straight to the fruits, taking one from the bowl which had much the same shape and colouring as an orange, skin which resembled that of a grapefruit, and a taste which seemed to encompass several familiar flavours, including those of the lemon, plum, and tangerine. 'Lovely,' he acknowledged.

'A multi-graft,' Arle explained. 'Our discoveries throughout the field of bio-genesis have made some remarkable graft-hybrids possible. Doctor Cher, our senior biologist, is ready to record a number of revolutionary findings on the subject of terrestrial plant mutation. But your interest, as I am well aware, runs in another direction.'

'I had rather imagined that yours might also,' Fisher returned, placing a spiky core on his plate and then sipping wine that reminded him of rarefied sunshine.

'Well, yes,' Arle conceded. 'But the occult is merely an extension of what we regard as the normal. Spirit for me equates psycho-plasticism, which in itself is the scientific basis of the imagination and the source of human creativity.

As creatures of matter, we are trapped

in the sphere of the semi-definable, and I have no use for truths that cannot be wholly pinned down.

'It is — as I hope has already been made clear to you, Mr. Fisher — your cast of mind that is so important to us. You have been granted moments of cosmic vision which are rare in Earth's breed of men. There is in you a capacity to bridge the gulfs of the galaxy and apperceive that life is not isolated to this one small world but is a phenomenon that is found at countless points among the stars. You have learned of those greater races — those seeders of the galaxy who no longer belong entirely to the material universe — and have come to accept that they, under God, have been given dominion wherever the new suns of the continuously expanding starfields appear. And out of your enlightenment comes the respect and sympathy for all life forms which is the mark of the truly advanced soul, on this world and every other. In our view, you are —

'A man for tomorrow,' Fisher put in flatly. 'I have heard it, sir. But don't expect miracles of me. I feel as ordinary as the next chap, and I'm no traitor to my own kind.'

'Let it be,' Arle cautioned. 'When you have slept.'

'Time enough,' Fisher agreed, setting his empty goblet aside.

'More wine?'

'No, thank you. I have had enough to eat and drink. And very good it was.'

'Let us hope that you will sleep well too,' Arle said. 'I will take you to your room.'

Fisher pushed back his chair and rose to his feet. He followed Arle back through the door by which they had entered the dining hall. They turned at once into a passage on the left. This had rooms situated on either side of it, and the bed that Fisher saw on looking through an open door told him that the older man and he had entered a dormitory area. Then Arle stopped and opened the way into a room on the right. 'You should be comfortable in here,' he said, stepping back and gesturing for Fisher to precede him across the threshold.

Entering, Fisher saw that the room was quite a small one. It contained a bed — which was set against the wall opposite the door — a table, a chair, and screened off toilet space. The floor was mostly bare plastic, but there was a purple carpet beside the bed and another of the same colour at the end of the room on the left, where the table and chair stood. For the rest, there was a plastic grille which covered the mouth of a ventilation duct which was situated in the wall just beyond the foot of the bed, and the light shone down from a cup of frosted glass in the ceiling. All that was necessary was present, but it was more than ever apparent that the Lexians took a spartan view of comfort.

'It will do nicely, sir,' Fisher said.

'Then,' said Arle from the doorway, 'I will leave you to your rest. Somebody will be sent to awaken you in the morning. You will be brought at once to me.'

Fisher nodded. They wished each other good-night. Then Arle withdrew and shut the door, and after that his footsteps faded in their return towards the dining hall.

Going to the bed, Fisher turned back the clothes and gave the mattress an experimental prod. It yielded in a manner that suggested it was made of a substance like foam rubber. He sat down on it, and removed his shoes, then got up again and stepped behind the screen, where he had a wash and otherwise made use of the toilet facilities. After that he returned to the bed, took off his jacket, trousers and shirt, folded them up and laid them aside, and then slipped into bed and stretched himself hard before relaxing, conscious now that, although he had been sparing with the wine, the drink was a strong one and the food which he had eaten had not been heavy enough to line his stomach against it.

Yawning, he let his eyes close; then, his mind fraying pleasantly, he considered rising and switching off the light; but, recognising the tomblike quality of the room, he decided to leave it burning, for the total darkness of a strange sleeping place could be a frightening circumstance in which to awaken. Then, as his mind filled with vaguely speculative matter and emptied again, sleep gathered him and dreams came.

He awoke sluggishly in the sweating, convulsive grip of nightmare. There was darkness about him, and it was that of a coffin. He forced himself up on his elbows, and, having a faint memory that he was far from home, tried to remember exactly where he was. Now he realized — the knowledge blasting all other — that he could hardly draw his breath and was choking. He fought his panic, trying to tell himself that the stifling fullness in his throat was only a symptom of hysteria, but the attempted rationalisation brought him no relief and, knowing that he was going to die if he didn't soon try to help himself, he rolled out of bed on to the floor and began crawling towards the spot where he believed the door to be, the bedside carpet gathering into a minor impediment under the clutch of his hands.

He found the wall opposite his bed. His fingertips brushed with the frantic, insensitive movements of the newly blind. He could feel nothing of the door; it ought to be there — but it wasn't. Had he been mysteriously transported in his sleep? Nonsense! Why wasn't the light still on then? Obviously because some fool had switched it off. Where was the door? He must think clearly. Left — right; it *had* to be somewhere nearby.

Then it occurred to him that, as the excluding feature in this airless room, the door must make a perfect fit with the stonework around it. Probably he had already touched the door a number of times but been unable to distinguish its surface from the polished granite of the wall. He must reach up higher: find the handle. Lungs roaring and scarlet lights beginning to flash in his brain, he heaved up on to his knees; then, his forehead pressing against the wall, he started feeling across the vertical surface before him with both palms, and a small cry of relief burst from his lips as the hand moving on his right fastened suddenly over the object he sought.

Recalling that the door opened

inwards, he screwed the handle round and then pulled, but nothing happened. Supposing himself mistaken in his original impression, he tried pushing instead, but again obtained no result. For an instant he became totally still. The door must be locked; that could be the only explanation of its refusal to open. He was a prisoner.

He banged on the door with his fists, but the actions were comparatively feeble, and the sounds that he created had little power to carry. The pressures in his chest grew unbearable, and the pulsing of the blood in his brain had put out most of the red lights and was tending to blackness. 'Help!' he croaked, banging still. 'Help!' But it was useless; nobody came. He was a captive — and something more.

He was a victim; there was a plan afoot to kill him. With the final clarity of a mind about to snuff out, he saw in the circumstances here the undoubted proof of it. The locked door, the darkness — they were the allies of an inflow of air that could only have been cut off deliberately. But why? — why? The

Lexians had gone to great trouble to single him out and transport him to this haven of theirs in the middle of Greenland. Had they — for any reason at all — wished to kill him, they could have had one of their agents carry out the crime in any one of a hundred different ways, or simply sat back and annihilated him in a flash of spontaneous combustion. It did not make sense. The Lexians had shown themselves capable of ruthless cruelty, yes; but only where an intelligent purpose seemed attachable to their crimes. To have brought him all this way just to murder him in a slow and sadistic manner related to no purpose that he could see.

It came to him then that things would not be so bad if he could just turn on the light. But all movement of that sort was now far beyond him. He toppled over on to his side; and then, as unconsciousness welled up and almost closed above him, he made an ultimate effort of will and began to crawl instinctively towards the ventilation duct which he had earlier noticed near the foot of his bed.

He found it without much difficulty. His fingers crooked through the grille, and it seemed to him that the tiniest whiff of oxygen entered his lungs. On the strength of it, he tried to raise himself again, muscles contracting violently, and the grille came away in his hands and he and it flattened before the mouth of the ventilator. Then, still driven by instinct, he hooked his fingers into the corners of the duct and dragged himself upwards until his head and shoulders collapsed into the aperture; and after that his senses left him — and it could have been death that gathered him in.

4

There was a tiny point of agitation in the blackness that became a renewal of thought. Fisher knew himself again. And then he became aware of areas of bodily discomfort that grew into pain. His chest felt bruised all through, his neck felt stiff, and there was a stinging in the upper part of his left arm. An enormous question-mark loomed inside his brain, but he could not yet recall why it should be there.

He opened his eyes, and heard himself let out a groan. There came an explosion of light through his retinas, and he rolled his head to the left and away from the blast. Then he remembered. There had been darkness before, and he had not been able to breathe. Well, now he could breathe again, and he was lying on a bed, which meant that he must have been put there — for had he not been crouched on the floor during those last moments?

— and there were figures standing around him, and he could also just make out the shapes of a mask and a pair of oxygen cylinders standing on a trolley nearby, and a table on which some medical instruments were laid out. 'Where am I?' he muttered; pointlessly, for he had already realized that he was still in the same room to which he had been led after eating in the dining hall of Project House.

Movement occurred at the foot of his bed. Fisher's gaze achieved full focus on it. He saw Arle standing there. The fleshy Khaka was present, too, his hands tucked into the sleeves of his robe and his face mandarin-like in its inscrutability. On the left of the pair were two more people: a man and a woman. The latter was young, and, allowing for those Lexian character-istics of eye and pigment and hair — which Fisher didn't find all that pleasing — rather beautiful. Light-boned, she was also very erect and proud — aristocratic; but there were also hints of warmth and kindness in her, and the melancholy loneliness of a dreamer who was slightly at odds with her environment. The man was old, small, wizened, and had a narrow, humourless quality, but he was deft of hand and sure of presence, and there was about his person a smell of antiseptic that marked him for the physician that he undoubtedly was. Now, as his gaze met Fisher's, he gave a sudden, pale smile which pinched off into a grimace, and then he turned his head and spoke a word which brought a nod of relief from the worried-looking Arle, who said: 'You have had a fortunate escape, Mr. Fisher. As well for you that you are still young and stronger than most.'

A fortunate escape. Why should that phrase strike so coldly? Then a shudder passed through Fisher. Somebody had tried to kill him. He remembered it all in detail now. The utter darkness, the choking sensations in a closed atmosphere which had given up all but its last vestige of oxygen — the locked door. But, as in the outcome it seemed unlikely that Arle had had anything to do with the attempt on his life — since you hardly attempted to slay a man in one minute and then tried to bring him back again in another — he imagined that the Project Chief saw the matter as he saw it and asked: 'Have you any idea why? — or who it could have been?'

'Who?' Arle looked genuinely puzzled. 'Why? I do not understand you.'

'Somebody — tried to kill me,' Fisher said, his hesitation arising out of the abrupt realization that Arle had placed a very different interpretation on what had happened to him from his own.

'This must all have been a terrible shock to you,' the Project Chief commented. 'Perhaps you were sleep-walking — possibly you were moving around the room in the dark in search of something. Whatever the explanation, you almost completely switched off the air-conditioning unit which is attached to the wall under the head of your bed. Mercifully, just sufficient air was still entering the ventilator to keep you alive once you had got your nose to the source. But even so, had my daughter Varinia' — he nodded towards the young woman who was standing next to the physician — 'not believed that she had heard sounds of knocking coming from this normally unused part of the building, and eventually become so uneasy about it that she came along to investigate, you could well have been dead before now and beyond all power of ours to help you. As it was, it was far from easy to bring you round.'

Fisher looked at the woman and spoke his thanks rather mechanically; and she, clearly understanding English, smiled and gave a nod that told him she was happy to have helped; but after that the Earthman switched his eyes quickly back to Arle and said: 'I tried to get out of the room when I awoke and found myself choking. The door was locked.'

'No,' Varinia said, the husky contralto of her voice carrying a rich thrill of maturity. 'The door was not locked.'

'Did you believe that you had locked the door before going to sleep?' Arle inquired.

'No,' Fisher replied. 'It never crossed my mind one way or the other. Besides, I had no means of knowing how.'

'The door has the most simple and

easily found of self-locking devices,' Arle said with a faint note of protest. 'It could be that you operated it, too, without knowing it. You have obviously been in a very confused state of mind.'

'Not that confused,' Fisher said firmly. 'I left the light on when I went to sleep, but when I awoke it had been turned off.'

'The light was off when I looked in,' Varinia said. 'It was the stifling condition of the atmosphere which made me realize that there was something wrong in here.'

'I believe,' Fisher went on deliberately, 'that somebody entered this room while I was asleep, switched off the air supply and the light — knowing that I was a total stranger to the fittings — and then went out and locked the door. I also contend that they returned at a later time, supposing me dead, and unlocked it again, believing, as has turned out to be the case, that you would put my fate down to a sleepwalker's misfortune or sheer carelessness on my part.'

'You are still alive, Mr. Fisher,' Arle reminded, glancing at his daughter. 'Varinia, did you see or hear anybody when you entered this part of the building?'

'No, father,' she answered. 'The area was deserted.'

'That may not be conclusive,' Arle said, 'but it ought to satisfy.'

'I stand by what I've said,' Fisher retorted.

Arle looked a trifle put out. 'You have no particular reason to trust us,' he admitted, 'but it would be a help to both parties if you could. We wish to go on treating you as a guest, but it will make it difficult for us to do so if you insist that there is a would-be murderer among us.'

'I do so insist,' Fisher replied.

'You are very important to us,' Arle said tightly. 'If you knew just how important, you would know what nonsense you are talking.'

'Let's analyse that,' Fisher said. 'Have you factions in this place? Could it be that all your people do not think the same way about me?'

Scowling, Arle appeared on the brink of making a really angry retort; but he held his words in check and his expression grew more thoughtful, a narrowed eye moving back and forth among his companions, as if he were inviting — or daring — some response on a subject to which those present were not after all strangers. However, no word came from Khaka, Varinia, or the physician, and Arle finally shrugged and said: 'Very well, Mr. Fisher. Two guards will be placed on your door. If you feel that curtails your freedom, remember that the fault is your own, and not ours.' Pointing at the medical instruments on the table, he gave the physician a curt order; then, beckoning to his daughter, he walked out of the room, Khaka following on behind the pair and casting the man on the bed a final glance that seemed a shade less inscrutable than heretofore and to contain little liking.

Fisher sighed inwardly, then turned his face to see what the physician was doing. He saw that the old man was preparing a hypodermic syringe. Then, the injection ready and the needle winded, the other reached for the Earthman's left arm, his head giving a reassuring nod. Fisher's immediate reaction was to refuse the injection — regardless of what it was or might do for him — but he knew that he had already made his feelings clear enough and saw nothing to be gained from being downright uncooperative in his mistrust, so he allowed the physician to thrust the needle into his arm and remained passive while its contents were forced into his bloodstream. After that he stared up at the ceiling, while the old man went out — leaving behind the trolley containing the oxygen cylinders and the table on which the medical instruments stood — then, as he became sure that the contents of the syringe had been a soporific, his eyes closed and he soon fell asleep.

He awoke, what seemed a long time later, to find himself receiving a bit of rough treatment. A Lexian was bending over the bed and alternately slapping his cheeks and shaking him. The man was young, wore one of the black and white uniforms, and had his forage cap tucked through his belt. Fisher frowned at the Lexian, then, after fending aside a further slap, he forced himself into a sitting position, a bilious sensation rising from his stomach and a stab of pain passing through his head. Then the room went into a slow, flat spin around him, and, fighting to quell his sickness, he felt more dreadful still. Unquestionably, his greatly disturbed night and the drugs used in his treatment were now taking their toll; but the uniformed man did not appear the least interested in his suffering, and pointed peremptorily to the foot of the bed, where his garments now lay, and Fisher was pretty sure that the Lexian would not forbear to throw him off the bed if necessary, which made him aware that the protective changes spoken of by Arle had led to an alteration in his status that was perhaps more radical than had been intended. Certainly it seemed that he was now being treated far more like a prisoner than a guest.

Getting out of bed, Fisher stood up shakily. He pulled on his shirt, trousers, and shoes. Then he lurched to the toilet facilities behind the screen, where he washed his face and neck in cold water, hoping to stimulate himself into a more normal state of health, but the chill of the liquid did very little for him, and he was shivering badly when he returned to his bed and there — still under the close eye of the uniformed man — put on and buttoned his jacket.

The Lexian motioned to the door. Fisher opened it and led the way into the passage beyond. Here Fisher saw another uniformed man standing, and realized that the other was the second of the guards whom Arle had said would be set to watch over him, the first being at his back. This second man seemed no more friendly than the first, and he gave Fisher a solid push to the left, guidance which the Lexian in the Earthman's wake extended by applying a solid palm between the shoulder-blades in such a manner as made him wonder where this toughening of attitude would stop.

The walk brought them to the dining hall. They entered it, and Fisher expected to see Arle there and to be offered another meal; but the echoing place was empty, and he was marched out through the door at its upper end. Now kitchen smells reached him from nearby, and he swallowed at his continuing queasiness. Then, after being steered through passages that were now completely unfamiliar to him, he came to the foot of a stairway much like that by which he had first descended into the basement, and a fifty step climb brought him back to ground level, where he was directed through the granite massivity of the upper corridors and brought to an open door through which he saw a lighted, windowless room in which Arle, Khaka, Doctor Samerle, and about twenty other important-looking Lexians of middle to advanced years were sitting at a fender-shaped table and showing traces of a rigid boredom that had almost certainly arisen from waiting much longer than had been anticipated for his appearance.

Fisher felt the hand drop from between his shoulder-blades as he stepped through the doorway and moved towards the table, noting now that a chair had been placed before the latter and that the Project Chief was already pointing towards it. 'Be seated,' Arle encouraged. 'How do you feel this afternoon?'

'Passable,' Fisher replied, sitting down, his forced smile giving the further lie to his state of incipient illness. 'I've been asleep that long?'

'Thirty six hours,' Arle answered. 'A long sleep is the best treatment for shock.'

Fisher did not try to conceal his surprise. So he had lost a day. No wonder he felt as he did. His condition must have been one of torpor at the time that he had been aroused. He supposed it was possible that the guard had been playing a much less unfriendly part than he had imagined in the degree of roughness used while waking him up. 'We come late to the explanation of my being in New Lexia,' he remarked.

'Any loss of time is to be regretted,' Arle observed somewhat enigmatically. 'We may have even less of it than the figures indicate.' He paused, his mouth tightening and his hard stare seeming to sum Fisher up anew; and then, slapping down his hands on the table before him, he sat sharply erect and went on: 'To business. You will have guessed who these men you see about you are. They are the most senior members of my project team, and the elders of our community. We will not go into the cataloguing of names and occupations; that would only amount to a further waste of time. Suffice it that your name, face, and attainments are known to everybody here. You and your progress among your own people have been watched for a number of years. Know, too, that all these men speak English. Being Earth's most favoured tongue, it has been obligatory for the more highly placed among us to learn it. You may be sure, then, that everything which passes here will be fully understood by everybody present.

'Very well. To tell you something of us. We are human, capable of interbreeding with the people of Earth, but in all respects far ahead of them. We come from a solar system which is situated at some distance from your own. From the sphere of the great star Altair in fact. That is to say, at about fifteen light years from this spot.

'Our galaxy teems with life, Mr. Fisher, and there are many worlds to which men may journey and find it; but, while the consciousness that we call life remains approximately the same — as between the different atomic bricks — individual life forms need widely different physical conditions in which to live naturally and thrive. Now, from one species to the next, these conditions are comparatively rare and make planetary migration a much less practicable proposition than might at first seem to be the case. I am saying that we Lexians have found only a few places beyond our own world where it is possible for our race to live, and that the Earth is by far the best of these because it so closely corresponds to Lexia, our home planet, in mass and atmosphere.

'Lexia, though not an old world, is a dying one. Its oceans have found their way through to the fiery materials which lie at the planet's heart. Over the last century this influx has created increasingly large seismic disturbances, and now the ultimate expansion of the internal gases is causing Lexia to reel on its axis. If the planet doesn't actually tear itself apart in a final explosion, it will certainly wipe all life from its surface with a last sequence of earthquakes and floods.

'This is a populous world, but our world is more so. Many must inevitably die in Lexia's climactic convulsions. It is, therefore, the duty of our ruling caste to save the best of our race. To that end, a big fleet of spaceships has been built on Lexia and stands on the spaceport near our global capital of Kredabah. We estimate that we can save a trifle over three hundred thousand of our best and cleverest. This may sound a large figure, but it is seen in its true perspective when you compare it with the population of a quite moderate city like Coventry, which has a count of more than three hundred and twenty thousand. Earth could absorb this tiny amount of extra population and never know the difference.' He smiled rather grimly. 'Yes, I have no doubt that you had guessed it. We wish to ask the nations of the Earth to give sanctuary to the elite of Lexia, and here and now we ask you to be our intermediary. The preservation of all things best in an alien civilisation should prove a cause in which you would make a fine advocate. In approaching the government of Great Britain, we began the conditioning of its members to think in terms of introducing you to the United Nations Assembly at the right time. We need you, and they need you. Yes, I expect you have also heard something like that before. The truth cannot help being obvious. Earth has everything to gain from us. Your space technology is a thousand years behind our own; and there is not one field, from the robotic to the sociological, in which we could not add vastly to the happiness of your peoples. Bearing all this in mind — and that you personally would not find us ungenerous friends once we had established ourselves among you — will you be our intermediary? Come now, Mr. Fisher, what do you say?'

'What do you say if I say no?' Fisher asked.

'It is better that we be strictly realistic about this,' Arle admitted gravely. 'The whole matter is too important to permit of our being otherwise. We Lexians are prepared to ask politely — we are prepared to plead our case if Earth insists on it — but in the last resort we are also prepared to fight. We have a base here that is more than large enough to hold the exodus from Lexia; and, as you are well aware, we also have a weapon that can heighten mollecular vibration and produce spontaneous combustion. This weapon, the fire-blaster, is capable of pinpoint accuracy at a range of thousands of miles — as we have occasionally demonstrated against wrong-doers, known and unknown, during the years of our hidden watch on your world. But the fire-blaster is only a minute portion of our capacity to harm. We have studied your machines and know how to disrupt their functions by the use of ultra-sonics, and we have also experi-mented with the Earth-bred mind and learned how to reduce nations to madness by the use of illusion and psychological horrors. To these purposes we set ourselves, without malice, and lifted away your machines and their crews from sky, land, and sea.' Arle's face had become very hard indeed, and there was a coldly challenging mockery in his stare. 'Well, Mr. Fisher, have you heard anything that you did not expect to hear?'

'Not a thing,' Fisher admitted.

'Knowing the facts, can you find room to blame?'

'No. If the situation were reversed, I expect our attitude would be much the same as yours.'

'Then you will help us?'

'I have no choice but to help you.'

Arle smiled, but the challenge was still present. 'You would be a real traitor to your own kind if you didn't, would you not?'

'My character and attributes mean very little to you,' Fisher said angrily. 'Any intelligent man would suit your purpose. You said yourself that you had given me no particular cause to trust you, and I don't. There is an element of force present, so how can there be perfect trust?'

Arle shrugged. 'I had supposed you broad enough of mind not to regard me as the final authority. I receive orders, and have to carry them out. The plan in which you find yourself the central figure was worked out on Lexia, and the great men who conceived it have commanded me to bring you to them. They have formulated the exact requests which they wish you to make to the United Nations, and they want to discuss them with you in order to make sure that you fully understand them. I see no need for this, but — ' He gestured his impotence in the face of his masters' orders. 'Our spaceship is being prepared to take you to Lexia. I shall travel with you; and my daughter is coming too. It will be her last chance to see the home planet that she has never seen. She was born here on Earth.'

'We are going to Lexia?' Fisher breathed disbelievingly. 'Didn't you speak of fifteen light years?'

The Project Chief nodded indifferently.

'You need not concern yourself with the time it will take. Once into warp, we travel outside time. Vastly beyond the speed of light. Because the normal time scale functions at either end of the journey, an exactly measurable time will elapse between our departure and our return; but nothing of it will be traceable to the flight itself. If you regard that as a mystery, it is one that neither I nor any clever man can explain to you. The mathematics of infinity are God's own; and His computer is the whole field of creation and all its suns.'

'How much time do I have to absorb this?' Fisher asked.

'You have a few hours,' Arle replied, an eye narrowing as he considered a clock that stood above a cupboard set in the wall on his right. 'Our ship will take off an hour or so after darkness has fallen. You need food and drink.'

'I need fresh air.'

'That you shall have,' Arle assured him. 'I expect you would like to see around New Lexia.'

'I would,' Fisher admitted, a note of

surprise in his voice; for, what with one thing and another, he had not supposed that he would be offered the chance.

'It has been arranged.' Arle called towards the door, speaking now, as Fisher saw on turning his head, to the guard who had brought him to this room, and the uniformed man bowed at last and marched off into what sounded like a return to the lower level of the building.

Wondering what precisely would happen next, Fisher sat with his hands in his lap. He looked towards the fender-shaped table as the men behind it began to mutter among themselves in their own tongue, and he felt uncomfortable as a number of sly glances were thrown in his direction. It was obvious that he was the centre of a certain amount of critical discussion, and he wished to goodness that Arle and company would throw in the occasional word of English; but he was not called upon to suffer the embarrassment of it for long, since footsteps again became audible in the corridor outside — this time dual and in a state of approach — and, twisting his head round again, Fisher saw the guard reappear in the doorway with Arle's daughter Varinia at his elbow. 'Go with my daughter,' the Project Chief said, smiling from Fisher to the woman. 'She will show you what there is to see.'

Fisher rose from his chair. He bowed to the New Lexian elders, then turned away and walked to the door, where Varinia met him with a hand that drew him to the left. After that she led him to a spot not far from the end of the corridor and opened a door that was built into a buttress. They passed through the exit into the light of day, and the woman closed up behind them; and then she moved towards a nearby concrete road at the nearer edge of which stood a small, beetle-shaped car, its perspex cover raised and standing open on its hinges to give immediate access to the twin seats behind its steering wheel and dashboard. 'Get in,' the woman said.

Reaching the car, Fisher climbed in and sat down in the passenger seat. Then Varinia got in also. She pulled the self-fastening cover down, brought the car's electric motor to life, and then eased the vehicle into motion. They rolled forward through the great shadow of Project House, the concrete road stretching whitely before them into the tree-obscured folds of a black-soiled distance.

But, once clear of the building on their right, there was much to see that was closer to hand. Other houses of granite were present. Most of them stood to the south of the road, but there were some to the north as well. Grey and massive — though much smaller than Project House — these buildings were linked by garden walks that ran between wide lawns and beds of flowers. Fountains, ornamental pools, statuary, follies, and summerhouses were also visible; and it seemed to Fisher that he saw in the scene a combination of the austere durability of Ancient Egyptian architecture and the delicate sophistication of Greco-Roman landscape gardening. There was nothing here of an alien nature to affront the Earth-bred eye, and Fisher had to accept that Arle's implied affinity between Earth and Lexia was, in this respect at least, a true one.

The road bore them beyond the built-up area. They passed between fir plantations and into the open land which lay beyond the trees. The black soil undulated gently, and the light which hovered above it was rose-yellow and hazy. Boulder and shrub and stream seemed softened by its touch. Fisher looked for the sun. It hung fairly low to the right of him — about where he had expected to see it in this early part of the winter season of the high latitudes in which he had been told that New Lexia was located — and it cast off a pearly glow into a gunmetal sky that blurred into a kind of faintly vibrating penumbra not far below it. 'The Lexian Shangri-la,' he mused aloud.

'Shangri-la?' his companion questioned.

'An imaginary sanctuary,' he explained, 'behind the storms and highest mountains of Tibet. It forms the background of a very famous story written by a man named James Hilton. In the Valley of Lost Horizon all the finest treasures of Art and the human spirit were to be preserved against the ultimate catastrophe.'

'It is an apt parallel,' Varinia agreed. 'We are trying to preserve all that is best of our Lexian civilisation.'

'But will you after all destroy us?'

'Of course not!' she protested. 'It is to eliminate all risk of that that you are here. I had hoped that my father would have made that abundantly clear to you.' As by an impulse, she made a right turn which took the car off the concrete road and on to a side turning that was no better than a dirt track. They began heading south at a much increased speed. 'I will take you to the place where storm and sunshine meet. It is, perhaps, the most interesting sight that I can show you.'

'Leaving aside the question of ecological damage,' he persisted, 'it would be your most effective way of dealing with us. Where I personally am concerned, there's a lot that does not make sense. I have just told your father as much. My excellences are supposed, in the context of the situation. Any intelligent and liberal-minded man would suit the Lexian purpose. My replacement would be easy; and that suggests that the attempt to kill me the night before last — which, logically, was an effort on somebody's part to clear the way for a violent policy towards Earth — has to be balanced against another party's so far hidden reason for bringing me here in the first place. Or perhaps I should not expect you to see that.'

'You doubt my father,' the woman said. 'I am sure that you can trust him, and you can certainly trust me. Your unfortunate experience in your room was an accident. You are using your intelligence destructively. You underestimate your worth. You are a very enlightened man. My race — and yours — will presently have cause to bless you.'

'I'd like to believe that,' Fisher said. 'I'm still sure there's something I can't come at in all this.'

'You have only to do your best,' she assured him, 'and all will be well.'

He nodded doubtfully. 'I understand we are to be travelling companions.'

'Yes,' she acknowledged, as increasingly less fertile tracts of land slid by on either side of the car. 'I am to see Lexia this one time, and to meet the Emperor.'

'This is the first I've heard of an Emperor.'

Varinia smiled, girlish in her sudden enthusiasm. 'You will meet him too. He is semi-divine, and the ruler of the whole of Lexia. When the planet of my ancestors dies, he will die with it; and the billions who must be left behind by the spaceships will meet their fates bravely because he is there to bless them with his presence and show them how to go.'

'Semi-divine?' Fisher queried. 'Well, if he means that much to his people, I suppose calling him semi-divine does no harm; but we Earth-people gave up an even half-credulous worship of our rulers long ago.'

'There has been a cheapening of your values over the last thirty years,' Varinia commented. 'We students of the televiewers have noted it. To give reverence to those worthy of it is an act that ennobles the lowliest.'

'I agree with you,' Fisher said — 'provided they *are* worthy of it. I've yet to hear of an emperor who was. It has been wisely said that all power corrupts, and absolute power corrupts absolutely.'

'That,' Varinia returned in tones that brooked no argument, 'is untrue of the glorious Tuga Halshafar. He is the most ascetic and holy of men. His rule is easy, his words are sage, and his example is irreproachable.'

'It seems to me doubtful whether I shall meet him,' Fisher said. 'I am to be vetted and coached on Lexia by men who have drawn up the requests that I am to make to the United Nations. I wouldn't expect to find your paragon of a ruler among them. Would you?'

'Perhaps not,' she admitted, slowing down with her eyes upon a boulder-piled embankment that reared above the ledge on which the road ran for a short space directly ahead of them. 'But that does not exclude your meeting the Emperor.'

He supposed that was true; but, seeing that the woman was wary of this particular part of the way, he said nothing more to distract her. Then, as they passed on to the road-bearing shelf, he appreciated the reason for her uneasiness; for, discounting any rocks that the vibrations of over-fast travel might bring down, there was a ditch on the left of them that had enough depth to ensure a nasty accident should they run off the edge of the road and fall into it.

But they soon cleared the danger area, and the woman picked up speed again. Fisher craned briefly in the direction from which they had come. He judged that they were now two or three miles beyond the spot at which they had turned off the concrete road. Here the sun had a much paler and colder appearance than when he had studied it from further back, and the shadow beneath it had several times the gloom and density that had been visible before. And then he saw the substance behind the penumbral presence. It took the form of a greyish-white wall that was over sixty feet high and reared more-or-less uniformly into the streak and flicker of windborne snow-flakes that flew in multitudes on the other side of an atmospheric barrier which instantly dissolved any icy shape which came into contact with it. 'How is it done?' Fisher asked in awe.

'Cyclic high pressure,' she replied. 'Our atmospheric units keep up a relay of warm airs, which begins and ends at the main plant to the east of us. By this means we have created an area of eternal summer in a district where the sun would normally be seen perhaps a dozen times a year.' She stopped the car about two hundred and fifty yards short of the great wall of ice and snow. 'When my father first came here,' she went on — 'some twenty years before I was born — the ground on which the car is now standing was covered by snow and ice to the depth of the wall you see before us. I have heard him say that it took a decade for the earth about us to clear and harden. Those early days must have been difficult ones for the members of my father's original team.'

'I can see that,' Fisher said, a genuine respect in his voice. 'What would happen if your atmospheric plant ceased to operate for a week, or even a day?'

'An hour would make a profound difference,' Varinia answered. 'Depending on the severity of the weather about us, this garden place would become an icy wasteland at the same rate as the atmospheric pressure within our circle dropped. But there is little chance of that happening. The system has sufficient back up plant throughout to take care of every foreseeable emergency. In more than forty years of operating time, there has never been a total failure yet.'

'In view of what you said before,' Fisher reflected wryly, 'that's encouraging. Used sensibly, atmospheric plants modelled on yours could reclaim a lot of valuable land from the grip of Boreas.'

'One more advantage that Earth could have of us,' she agreed. 'Have you seen enough?'

Fisher nodded. There was a disturbing subjectivity — almost something unnatural — about the scene beyond him that made it better taken in small doses.

Varinia turned the car round. Then she began driving back in the direction of the concrete road. She told him that she was going to show him some of the croplands next. He said that that would interest him; but his thoughts were really on a different matter; for it had come back to his mind that somewhere in New Lexia was a place where the machines and crews stolen from the outside world were kept. He could, of course, do nothing for the prisoners at present, but he wondered whether it would be possible to speak with them; and he was still pondering as to whether or not it would be basically wise to broach the subject to Varinia, when he saw that they were again nearing the embankment with the rocks on its summit and the section of the road which ran parallel to it on the shelf with the ditch at its base.

The car was about twenty yards from the ledge, when Fisher looked up. In that instant he saw a movement among a precariously balanced cluster of boulders at a nearer part of the embankment's front edge. Then one of the largest rocks started to roll outwards and down, jostling smaller portions of stone into a minor avalanche that was obviously going to shatter the car if it went on moving straight ahead. There simply wasn't time to shout a warning at his companion. He seized the steering wheel and spun it to the right. The car shot off the road and went bumping down a piece of rough, steeply sloping ground into the ditch under the ledge, where he turned it in as close against the vertical rock on his left as he could get it.

Varinia disengaged the drive for herself. Then Fisher pushed her down over the steering wheel and bent his upper body above hers, praying that he had got the placement of the vehicle as nearly right as possible, and after that he heard the first of the rocks crash down on the road above them and glimpsed the ominous shadow of a bounding mass that could mean annihilation. In a split second from now they would know how it was to go.

5

Fisher felt an incalculable relief as the boulder leapt clean over the car, struck the back of the opposite lip of the ditch, and then toppled away into the hollow which lay beyond. Clearly, the rock had fallen far enough to produce a good bounce on the road above, and he experienced a further lightening of his fears as more and more of the larger elements from the avalanche sprang above the sheltering vehicle and went the same way as the first.

In a matter of seconds — that seemed like hours — the showering of the rocks came to an end. Fisher straightened instantly, conscious that the crisis was by no means over, and tipped back his head to stare directly upwards through the transparent roof of the car. He saw boulders piled up to and over the edge of the shelf above him, and then he perceived that one was poised on top of the rest in a very menacing position indeed. Scree and dust were trickling and blowing away from the shifting stones that supported the threat, and it was clear that collapse and the fall of the uppermost rock on top of the car could not be long delayed. 'Don't pause!' he urged, as Varinia switched on the motor again and cast a doubtful eye towards the steep and rutted climb about thirty yards before them which offered the only progressive way out of the ditch. 'Just get out of here!'

With her hands shaking but her mouth firm, the woman engaged the drive and turned away from the previously protecting wall, the vehicle's perspex cover grinding and flawing from a moment of over-tight contact with the stone; and then she sent the car nosing rapidly out of harm's way, and it reached the end of the ditch and turned up the slope there at the exact instant that the poised boulder thudded down in its wake and brought a shower of stones and smaller debris with it, the whole forming a mound that would have flattened and buried the frail vehicle if it had failed to get away in time.

Varinia went to full power as the car reached the sixty degree slant at the middle of the ascent. The machine hesitated, hung shrilling for a particle of time, then picked up and went rocketing into the second half of the climb, its speed carrying it over the top of the slope in a half-controlled wobble which became a vicious snake as it tipped back to the horizontal and headed in the general direction of the road beyond.

By skilful use of brake and wheel, the woman regained full control of the car and showed every sign of rejoining the road and going straight on; but Fisher couldn't stand for that, since he was sure in his heart that the avalanche had been man-made and another attempt at murder. 'Stop!' he ordered. 'Let me out!'

Pale and frowning, the woman brought the car to a halt at the edge of the road, and, the question large in her gaze as she turned her face towards him, released the catch that held the cover in place and stepped out as she lifted the transparent cup and left it standing in its open position.

Fisher sprang up and jumped clear of the vehicle. Then he crossed the road and ran towards the slanting rear of the nearby embankment. Reaching a position from which he could see down the entire length of the formation's back, he made out a man on the more distant part of the lower acclivity. The other was slightly built and dressed in the white knee-length robe and trousers that seemed to distinguish New Lexia's upper class from the men in the black and white uniforms who did the more menial forms of work.

Seeing Fisher, the Lexian threw himself into motion and pelted off the slope. Fisher immediately changed course to the right and sped down a line of interception. He saw that the would-be murderer was making for a depression that was about three hundred yards from where his run had started, and, as the pair of them converged on the sunken ground, Fisher perceived hidden in its depths a small version of a flying saucer. Obviously the Lexian had earlier used the flying machine to watch the progress of Varinia's car from the air, and had settled towards the ambush point while the woman and the Earthman had been looking at the boundary area in which New Lexian summer and the worst of arctic weather had their meeting place. Well, since the other was one of the senior breed, it was probable that he could speak English, and if he could do that, it should prove possible to shake out of him exactly what was going on.

Plainly out of condition, the Lexian's movements became ragged as he neared the depression's edge. Fisher increased his own speed, then dived forward and brought the man down on the brink of the bowl itself. They rolled together, Fisher losing his grip as the other jerked a knee into his chest, and then they rolled apart. The Lexian jumped to his feet ahead of the Earthman, and, pulling up the hem of his robe, snatched a pistol-shaped weapon out of the top of his trousers. He pointed it at the rising Fisher and pressed the trigger, miniature lightning striking from its muzzle and just missing the Earthman's head. He shifted his aim to release another shock, but Fisher reached him ahead of the discharge and knocked the weapon aside with his right forearm, hooking with his left fist. The blow landed with perfect timing, and the Lexian dropped cleanly before it and lay unstirring on his face.

Stepping back, Fisher set his hands on his hips and fought a minute-long battle to regain the breath that he had lost; then, feeling able once more, he bent forward and picked up the weapon from the ground. Turning it over, he was in the act of examining its battery and coils, when he heard a commanding shout from his back and craned to see two men in black and white uniforms running towards him from a car which they had left parked beside the road close to the spot where Varinia's vehicle was still standing motionless.

Desisting from the examination, Fisher now kept one eye on the man lying before him and the other on the pair coming up. They reached him just as the felled Lexian gave vent to a groan and showed signs of recovering consciousness. Fisher recognised them as the two men who had been responsible for guarding his room. The one who had not so long ago conducted him to the council room snatched the shock-pistol out of his hand and pointed towards Varinia's car in a manner that said go — or else!

Fisher twitched a shoulder. He supposed the pair had been lying in the background all the time. He could not tell with certainty how much they had seen of what had happened here, but the amount must have been in his favour — for there was obviously no question of their resenting what he had done to the man lying on the ground — so he left them without more ado and trotted back to where Varinia was still standing beside her car. 'Did you see the face of the man I knocked down?' he asked.

She nodded glumly. 'His name is Dareus. He is an electronics engineer from Khaka's global watch.'

'Anything else? He tried to kill us, you know.'

'Nothing that could help. The ergo-men will attend to it.'

'So that's what you call them,' Fisher said. 'I would not describe those two as the most friendly people I've ever met. I believe we're required to drive on.'

They got back into the car and she pulled the cover down. Then she set the vehicle in motion and drove back on to the road, accelerating once she had its slightly smoother surfaces under the wheels and had passed the car which had brought the two uniformed men to the spot. Fisher looked back. He saw one of the ergo-men helping the man whom he had knocked unconscious towards the car that Varinia had just put behind them, while the other was moving into the depression in which the miniature flying saucer lay, probably with the intention of flying it back to wherever it had set out from.

Then Varinia said: 'So there really are those among us who want to take over the Earth by war.'

'And badly enough to take your life in order to get mine.'

'I am only a woman, Mr. Fisher. The Lexians do not have too deep a concern for their females. The game here is a man's game.'

'At least there's no mistaking its presence now. By the way. My first name is Craig. Please call me that, and, if I may, I'll call you Varinia.'

'Do,' she said. 'I'm sorry that we doubted you. You can rely on my father to bring the guilty into the open and punish them.'

'Yes, Dareus didn't strike me as the type to be a lone operator. Have you any idea who the guilty may be?'

Varinia hesitated, then said rather lamely: 'They might be almost anybody, Craig. To be honest with you, there is hardly a man in New Lexia who at some time or the other has not said that the subjugation of Earth would make the best answer to our problems.'

'That's as I expected, Varinia,' Fisher acknowledged.

'But in every case — or almost every case — better sense has later prevailed,' the woman went on. 'The nations of the

Earth are inferior to us in the destructive power of their weapons, but we could not really hope to put down a population of more than three and a half thousand millions without exposing ourselves to terrible risks in the process.'

'We have the atomic bomb,' Fisher agreed, 'and we have intercontinental ballistic missiles capable of reaching any spot on the globe. Once New Lexia had been located — and your continuous activity would ensure that happening pretty soon — you would be placed under heavy bombardment from all around the compass. It would be virtually impossible for you to keep track of every missile launch, and it would need only one atomic warhead to get through to raze your atmospheric plant and create the kind of conditions that would force any survivors under the ground.'

'I regard the risks as unacceptable,' she admitted. 'But I also insist that we are a moral race who much prefer to do things the proper way.'

There he considered that she was to some extent nourishing another delusion, but he realized that it would not be friendly at this stage to remind her of the facts — emphasized by his earlier thinking and his now firm decision not to mention those captives from the outer world who must be somewhere here present — which proved the Lexians no less fundamentally amoral and opportunist than any other race in the human family; so he let her words be the last on the subject for the time being and looked ahead to where the concrete road was visible again, betting with himself that Varinia would see in their recent experience the cancellation of her commission and turn back to Project House. But he lost the bet, for, on coming to the road, she turned right in the most prompt of manners and began heading again into the eastern quarter of New Lexia, where they soon came to fields of green corn, wet acres of paddy, and bumper plantings of edible roots. Robot farm equipment seemed to be doing most of the work in progress, and Varinia told him that, by the use of the most intensive agricultural methods yet devised, her people reckoned to gather three harvests annually. She also explained how they got most of their animal protein from the moose and reindeer herds which had wandered into the area across the years, and rounded off their diet with green plants of the lettuce-cabbage variety and the copious products of their orchards.

The croplands were rather more than two miles wide. They ended at a low ridge which had been breached by a cutting that carried the road. On the other side of the ridge, the car and its two occupants were confronted by a huge building with blunt, square chimneys and mushroom-shaped vents that pointed their heads horizontally to north and south. The woman said that the works ahead were the home of the atmospheric generators and that the eastern border of New Lexia was only a short distance beyond them. His curiosity at a peak, Fisher thrust his head forward and waited for them to move right up to the plant, but then they arrived at an intersection — which was situated short of any real detail becoming visible — and Varinia turned off to the left and began following another concrete road northwards, thus leaving her passenger completely unsatisfied in his desire to get a closer look at the strange building.

They came to a cemetery next. It was a place of small brick tombs and no monuments. There was but one hint of funeral pomp about it. This took the form of an arched gateway that had been constructed out of white tusks that were huge and magnificiently curved. Fisher whistled his awe of them, and was told that they had come from the remains of several mammoths that had decomposed at the first touch of the sun after reposing in the glacier that had previously covered this part of New Lexia for hundreds of thousands of years. Varinia also pointed out her mother's tomb, and then spoke briefly but fondly of the young student who had journeyed to Earth on a Lexian State Scholarship — intending to return after three months and continue her education at home — but who had stayed behind to be the wife of a man even then old enough to be her father and had died giving his daughter birth. It had been a sadness, so Varinia said, from which Arle had never fully recovered; and it was clear that she deeply regretted never having known her mother.

The cemetery behind them, they veered away from the borderland and came to a populous industrial complex. Here, Varinia explained, all the manufacturing necessary to New Lexia was carried out. Everything from a shoe to a flying saucer could be constructed in the buildings that formed a dark fan-shape on their left. True, many new designs and inventions — along with their machine tools — were imported from Lexia itself, but the Earth colony could otherwise claim to be as industrially self-supporting as it was in every other way.

They went on for another mile or two, the bend of their path carrying them into New Lexia's northern territory, and it was here that Fisher saw a sight which quickened his heart. For a frowning mound of great size broke the flattish line of the horizon and turned the face of a black and slightly receding cliff towards them, the rock presenting the largest of closed doors to the inner lands of the aliens' circle and suggesting that all kinds of secrets might be hidden within its mass. And Fisher felt an intuitive prompting that here was the place where the machines and crews lifted from the outside world were kept in an isolation that probably resembled a living death. Seeing now an extensive black runway before the doors in the rockface — and remembering what had happened at the approaches to the atmospheric plant — he said as casually as he could: 'I'd like to go closer.'

'I am sorry,' Varinia replied. 'It is forbidden.'

Despite his recent decision concerning the captives, her tone provoked him, and he asked: 'Why?'

'I cannot discuss it.'

'I think I can guess the reason why.'

'Then why ask it?'

'If we are to be one people — '

'We are not one people yet,' she interrupted.

'A gesture of goodwill on your part might not be a bad thing.'

'We cannot have aggressive aliens upsetting our work here with their plots and imaginings.'

There, she had divulged the fact of it for herself. 'You'd blame them?' he asked stiffly. 'Remember who the real aliens are.'

'You are being provocative, Craig Fisher.'

'I can't help seeing the facts as they are. Whatever your needs, the wrong is all with you Lexians.'

'We have wronged but a few of you,' Varinia returned defensively.

'The few are the factor of the many.'

'A few threads may have to be sacrificed to the larger design. My father always says as much.'

'I refrained from saying this before,' Fisher said. 'By what right do you regard yours as a highly moral race?'

'I have said too much,' Varinia said self-reproachfully. 'Things are as they must be. You must look elsewhere for a perfect situation.'

'Good,' Fisher remarked shortly. 'We're being fully realistic again.'

'Yes,' she agreed, glancing to her left and skywards, a touch of grim humour in the pursing of her lips. 'Here comes one of the symbols of that reality.'

Surprised for the instant, Fisher looked up and saw that she was referring to a miniature flying saucer — a craft that was identical to the one which he had seen near the Lexian who had tried to crush them under the rockfall — which was swooping in from the south. Then, moments later, it landed about two hundred yards ahead and on the right-hand side of the road, and the machine's pilot — an ergo-man — opened a sliding hatch in its cupola and jumped out, waving for the car to stop, and Varinia slowed down and then halted beside the pilot, who gave her a respectful smile as she lifted the vehicle's top and then spoke to her for several seconds in the Lexian tongue, his words resulting in a nod from her and an immediate resumption of the car's movement. 'We have to return at once to Project House,' Varinia explained, as the uniformed man's bowing presence slipped to the rear. 'I was going to show you the spaceship that will take us to Lexia, but the interrogation of the man who tried to push the rocks down on our car is waiting on our appearance, so we shall have to forego the rest of our tour.'

'I suppose it has to happen so soon because we are leaving for Lexia tonight,' Fisher observed.

'That must be it,' she agreed.

Before long they came to another intersection in New Lexia's sparse road system. Varinia made a left turn and headed down the edge of the western land for which they had been making. The speed of the electric car built to its maximum, and in a minute or two the scattering of buildings of which Project House was the main one appeared before them. The woman slowed down again as she neared the granite loom of the chief structure, and then she turned into the road on its northern side and brought the car to a stop beside the door from which they had left at the beginning of the trip.

An ergo-man appeared at once from the doorway. He stood by while Varinia and Fisher got out of the car. Then, with a single word, he faced about and re-entered the building, and Fisher and the woman followed him through the door and the gloom of the corridor beyond it, the man's lead bringing them again to the windowless council room with the fender-shaped table, where Arle sat in the middle and only chair now occupied on its length and Khaka stood as a brooding presence at his back, while Dareus, the would-be killer, and his three guards stood inside the left arm of the table and Doctor Samerle, wearing a pointed red cap of the wizard style and carrying what looked like a black wand of office, faced them across the floor from inside the right.

Then, as Fisher and Varinia came to a halt directly before him and at the centre of the room, Arle glanced at the Earthman and said: 'My apologies, Mr. Fisher. You seem to have been right, and I wrong. There is a threat to your life. At least we apprehended it this time.'

'Your daughter was in danger too,' Fisher reminded.

Arle nodded. 'I will hear her account of

it. In our own tongue, if you please, Varinia.'

The woman began to speak, and, though it was apparent that she was not pressing her account in any spirit of malice, her words were clearly so damning that the prisoner's face grew paler and more despairing by the moment. Then, after Varinia had concluded what she had to say, Doctor Samerle stepped forward and tapped Dareus on the crown with his wand — perhaps enjoining truth — and began asking questions in bullying tones, but not one of these was answered, and he finally stepped back to his original position, quivering with anger, and deferred to Arle, who glanced round and up at Khaka, asking a question of his own, which was answered with a sombre finality which set the prisoner literally shaking at his knees.

Next Arle spoke to the still hovering man who had brought Varinia and the Earthman into his presence. The other turned aside and went to the cupboard which was situated on the right of the room as seen from the chairman's seat. Opening it, the man took out a cabinet of some lightweight plastic substance that was six feet six inches tall and carried it to a spot near the prisoner, where he set it down on the floor and opened the door in the front of it, revealing a smooth-walled emptiness that was as innocent-looking as any ever displayed at the exposure of the interior of a magician's trick cupboard.

'Yes,' Arle agreed in English, as if he had once more been reading Fisher's mind, 'it appears the most innocent of objects. Yet it has never failed to get the truth out of even the bravest and most recalcitrant of prisoners. Dareus here has refused to answer the official interrogator's questions concerning his accomplices in the commission of his crime.

Thus he must face the terrors of his own deepest mind in the strange dimensions of the Cabinet of Kalthar. Having once met his personal demons face to face, a man is always willing to give a truthful account of all he knows in order to obviate a second meeting.' Gesturing towards the cabinet, he then barked out a command, and two of the guards seized the prisoner and forced him backwards into it, Doctor Samerle moving to the front again and standing in close proximity to the man for a long moment before shutting the door on him and fixing its catch.

There was a withdrawal from the floor immediately about the cabinet. The guards halted at spots on the left and right of it, while Samerle stopped his backing at a point about nine feet from the tall object and folded his arms, his wand jutting upwards out of a cramped left hand and his features betraying signs of tension.

For a few seconds there was a general silence and no movement came from the cabinet; then an ominous gurgling noise issued from it and there was a bodily slump within that caused it to shudder where it stood. Grunting, Arle shot out of his chair and bent across the table, his weight resting on his palms and his expression telling that the things which had just happened were no part of what he had expected. Then he made a sign to the guard standing nearest to him, and the man jumped to the cabinet and opened its door, the unfortunate Dareus pitching out of it and coming to rest on his right side on the floor, a pungent dribble issuing from the corner of a mouth in which the teeth were tightly bared. It needed no physician to pronounce the man dead, and it was likewise easy to see that he had died of poison. Then Arle made angry demands of the guards in the Lexian tongue, and, influenced by the Project Chief's tone of voice, Fisher asked of Varinia: 'Wasn't Dareus searched before he was brought in here?'

'That is what my father was just asking,' she replied, listening as one of the guards answered her parent. 'Yes, he was searched — for poison as well as other things — and thoroughly.'

Doctor Samerle knelt beside the body, and, careful not to touch the spittle that was still leaking from the jaws of the corpse, turned Dareus on to his back and forced his mouth wide open, peering quickly but carefully around its interior and finally looking up to make a statement that caused Arle to let out a sigh of frustration and drop back heavily into his chair.

'A hollow tooth,' Varinia explained. 'He had a capsule of poison secreted in a hollow wisdom tooth.'

'I see,' Fisher said, though he didn't at all; for he simply could not imagine any man being able to keep enough poison to kill him more or less instantly in a tiny cache of quite such dubious security. However, as Arle appeared satisfied that it had been as Samerle had said, there seemed nothing to gain by questioning it, and Fisher looked on in a far from happy silence as the guards picked up the body and carried it out, Doctor Samerle walking behind them.

'A pity,' Arle said, when all sound of the retreating men had faded. 'The Dareus I knew was a good fellow. That he should have been ready to attempt murder must indicate the depth of the division that lies between my sensible, peace-loving majority and the crazy few.'

He gnawed his lower lip, and gave his head a shake. 'If only we could have made him talk. It would have gone far towards putting matters right. But it serves no purpose to bewail the silence of the dead. I shall be pleased when this day is over and we are aboard the spaceship. You should be safe there, Mr. Fisher.'

'One hopes so,' Fisher said.

Arle grimaced at his daughter. 'Take him down to his room, Varinia. Stay with him. There are a few things I must discuss with Khaka. After I have done that, I will join you both.'

The woman inclined her head. She began moving towards the door, and Fisher started after her; but he had not walked far, when a thought came to him with such force that it stopped him in his tracks and caused him to swing round again and say: 'You will have the spaceship searched for possible sabotage, sir? It occures to me that the men who would risk killing Arle's daughter in order to kill me might not be too particular about killing Arle himself in the same cause. There could be as much ambition in this as the forcing of hands.'

'The possibility had not escaped me,' Arle answered in a voice that was far more astringent and dismissive than had previously been the case. 'The spaceship has been searched, will be searched, and then searched again.'

Fisher felt that he had been rebuked. He swung on his heel and strode to where he saw Varinia waiting for him in the doorway. Then they continued with withdrawal, and she soon led him down the stairs that gave access to the eastern end of the basement, on through the dining hall, and then beyond it into the dormitory area where his lodging was situated. After that they entered his room and he saw that the bed had been made and a lot of tidying up done. Pointing to the chair, he asked the woman to sit down, and, as she did so, he lowered himself on to the bed and avoided her eye, frowning to himself as he heard two guards take up their places outside the door and a number of more distant sounds which suggested that others were now watching the dormitory area from either end of the passage on which his room stood. He supposed the increased security was inevitable, but it made him feel more hemmed in than safe, for it seemed to him that his status still possessed a variable factor.

After that a time of silence and inactivity began. He tried to think of something to say, but, despite all that had happened to them recently, nothing would come, and he soon suspected that Varinia was having the same difficulty. They sat inert and stared at the walls, and the atmosphere tremored around them and emphasized the state of negation.

It must have taken Arle much longer to conclude his business with Khaka than he had believed would be the case when he had spoken of joining the Earthman and Varinia, for it was well over an hour later when he entered Fisher's room. After eyeing his daughter and her companion and picking up their inertia, he stirred them with the whiplash of his mind, and before long he had them arguing about the scientific and economic problems of an Earth/Lexian future which he appeared to see with a startling clarity, and it seemed that some remarkable possibilities were coming through when he suddenly clapped his hands and brought the talk to an end, announcing that it was time that they ate and made ready for departure.

They left the room and went along to the dining hall, where a meal of trout, Arctic goose, veal, and fruit had been set out for them; and, his stomach now feeling settled and ready to take account of how long it had been empty, Fisher ate well and drank enough wine to put him in the kind of relaxed mood that he knew he must watch. Sitting on his either hand, his companions also made a good meal; then, after allowing a few minutes for digestion, Arle rose from the table and said that it was time they made their way to the spaceport; and they left the basement and walked out through the buttress door into the newly fallen night.

A large electric car was standing at the edge of the nearby road. Its nose pointed to the left, and a driver was already sitting behind its steering wheel. Arle got into the vehicle and sat down beside the driver, and Fisher and Varinia seated themselves behind the pair a moment later. Then the driver set the car in motion, and he drove his passengers westwards over New Lexia's starlit landscape and into an area where broken patterns of incandescence marked the presence of a major installation that Fisher thought must be the Project's spaceport. It was soon obvious that this was indeed the case, for, as they neared the lights, buildings took shape among them, and then the rearing presence of a still greater form became apparent amidst the white brilliance of some loading arcs, and Fisher traced the bullet-nosed, fin-broken silhouette of a spacecraft that was five hundred feet tall and otherwise had the dimensions of a small ocean liner.

The car stopped at the rear of what appeared to be the terminal building. Arle and his companions left it, the ergo-man driver standing to attention for them. They passed into the big building adjacent and Fisher found himself in a nicely appointed lounge, where Khaka and Doctor Samerle rose to greet them from a leather settee and pleasantries were exchanged, though these ended with Khaka speaking a more serious word in Arle's ear and Doctor Samerle picking up a silver cage from a shelf nearby and holding out it and the multi-coloured, saurian-crested bird it contained to Varinia, a song of the utmost sweetness coming from the bird at that moment and filling the lounge with an almost unbearable melancholy. 'It is for the Emperor,' Samerle said in English. 'Please give it to him, Varinia. I remember how well he used to love the song of the Cassiaboa. The bird is, so I have been told, now extinct on Lexia, and its song only a memory. To hear again the melody of the summer gardens of yesteryear will make the hours of the last cataclysm that much more bearable for him.' There were tears on the doctor's cheeks. 'You will do this little thing for him and me, my dear?'

'Of course, Doctor,' Varinia said, a break in her own voice as she took the cage from the other's hand. 'You honour me.'

Samerle bowed until his forehead almost touched his knees. 'Thank you, child. Assure the Emperor that I will remain his devoted subject forever.'

'That I will also do,' Varinia promised him kindly.

Arle gave the doctor a sympathetic pat on the shoulder, then, following up with a smiling nod for Khaka and a jerk of his head at Fisher, took his daughter by the arm and led her out through the glass doors in the room's western wall, the Cassiaboa bird singing again as they stepped into the light-streaked darkness beyond.

Fisher followed father and daughter on to the spaceport's apron. Then he heard a call and discerned a man standing on a trolley-like conveyance a few yards ahead of them. Arle and Varinia climbed on to the trolley's platform, and Fisher stepped up behind them, the vehicle moving off instantly and making for the mighty spaceship, which could now be seen in some detail about half a mile to the west.

The driver stopped the trolley in the spacecraft's immediate shadow and next to the floor of an elevator which obviously served a glowing hatch that was visible in the side of the vessel about a hundred feet above their heads. They stepped on to the ten square feet of the elevator's floor; then, as the lifting mechanism began to operate, Arle leaned towards Fisher and quietly said: 'Every part of the ship has been searched four times over. Khaka has just assured me that there is no possible chance of sabotage. I can personally vouch for the trustworthiness of every member of the crew. You have nothing to fear while we are in space, and I have already made arrangements to have you thoroughly guarded once we have reached Lexia.'

'Look,' Fisher said, the words welling out of him under the sudden pressure of a form of desperation that he realized must have been gathering in him for some time, 'I don't believe in this intermediary business any more. What's your real purpose in taking me to Lexia?'

But the elevator had reached the top of its ascent, and Arle was pleased not to hear. The Project Chief's hand was already joining that of a rangy, wide-browed Lexian who had just entered those early middle years which could be described as the end of youth. The other wore one of the familiar black and white uniforms, but his cuffs and collar were edged with silver braid and he carried four red bars on the breastpocket of his coat. A strong figure in the light of the hatchway, and separated from the men standing in the corridor at his back by an obvious deference, this man was clearly the captain; and, having talked with Arle for a moment or two on the threshold, he turned to the men behind him and issued a string of orders; then, as they hurried off, he moved towards the ship's interior on their heels, making it possible for Varinia and Fisher — who had been isolated on the elevator until then — to move into the hatch as Arle advanced in the direction that the crewman had gone, and for the automatic closure of the door at their rear.

The pair joined up with Arle again, and then the three were met by an ergo-man who had the subservient mannerisms of a steward. The newcomer conducted them through a number of shining passages and into the heart of the ship. Here he took them to a short and rather exclusive-looking corridor which had just three cabins which opened off its left-hand side. It was made clear that they were to be quartered here for the flight. Arle took the further of the three rooms, Varinia the middle one, and Fisher that which was nearest to the main corridor which served the area. Then the ergo-man went away, and, speaking from the doorway of his cabin as the Earthman and Varinia were about to shut themselves in, Arle said: 'It would be wise to lie down until the ship has cleared the Earth's gravitational field. A vessel of this size has to pass into free space before it can go into warp. If it did otherwise, it would probably carry several acres of the planet's surface with it.'

Calling thanks for Arle's advice, Fisher closed his door. He saw attached to the wall opposite a white bunk which lay in a deep metal tray which was roofed over at a height that would not impede the entering or leaving of it. Removing his shoes, he walked across to the bunk and climbed into it, lying down on his back and letting his gaze rove over the padded lid above him. Then he turned his eyes back into the cabin, and saw that it was just as simple as his accommodation at Project House had been. There was a table that folded into the wall near the door, an upright chair made out of plastic and tubular metal, a washbasin and a mirror. One object more could be seen. This was a video screen that was without visible controls and let into the wall beyond the foot of the bunk. Altogether, the spartan streak in the Lexian make up was again very apparent here.

An alarm began to bleep through a hidden loudspeaker. Fisher assumed that lift-off was imminent. Relaxing, he prepared himself to face whatever the experience held. The warning soon fell silent. Then power began to tremble through the ship. After that the great vessel shuddered detectably into the first stage of flight and settled into a climb that held Fisher's back firmly against the mattress beneath him. Despite his efforts to remain slack, he found himself clenching his fists harder and harder, and the thudding of his heart echoed unnaturally through his thoracic cavity. The minutes went by, and then came a moment when everything seemed to grow misty and lose form, but normality soon returned, and before long feelings of lightness and peace filled him and he became sleepy. It was all very comfortable; but then there burst upon him an intuitive imagery of the most startling and vivid kind as an all-important fact and a major inconsistency seemed to twine themselves together and point to the near certainty that the spaceship and everybody aboard it was in mortal danger.

Heaving himself out of his bunk, he headed for the door. There was no telling how much — or how little — time he had left.

6

Passing out of his cabin, Fisher swung along the passage to his left and banged on Varinia's door, entering unbidden and long before the sound of his knocks had ceased echoing. The woman was sitting at her table, Doctor Samerle's gift to the Emperor standing before her, and the caged Cassiaboa bird was singing as sweetly now as it had done back at the spaceport. 'Varinia,' he gasped, as she looked round and up at him, her face startled, 'You've got to get rid of that cage as fast as you can!'

'Have you gone mad?' the woman demanded.

'Indeed!' came Arle's confirmatory rumble, as he pushed in at the Earthman's back. 'What do you mean by bursting in on my daughter like this? Your hammering must have been heard in the control room itself!'

'I'm sorry,' Fisher returned, if only to

calm the other out of further time-wasting outbursts. 'I'm almost certain the base of the birdcage contains a bomb which may shortly blow us all to Kingdom Come.'

'Samerle's gift to Tuga Halshafar!' Arle cried, his tones at once horrified and full of incredulity.

'His gift to the devil!' Fisher retorted. 'Samerle told you that Dareus had concealed poison in a hollow tooth. It's more likely that the doctor slipped Dareus the fatal dose by a piece of sleight of hand. He was also in the position to know that this spaceship was to be thoroughly and repeatedly searched for signs of sabotage before leaving Earth, and that only the V.I.P. passengers themselves were likely to be missed by the search and be able to carry a bomb aboard. Why did he break form and use English when he spoke to Varinia of his wish to have her carry his gift of a singing bird to the Emperor? It could only have been because he wanted me to be influenced by the sad facts of his gift and, because of them, not to be suspicious of it. Your own language had covered everything that didn't directly concern me until then. Isn't that so?'

'It is so,' Arle admitted, the rasp in his voice telling how unwillingly he had allowed himself to be influenced by the Earthman's arguments; and, elbowing Fisher aside, he stepped up to the table at which his daughter sat, picked up the cage, and, regardless of the discomfort caused to its fluttering and now silent inmate, turned it over until he could look directly at its base. 'The screws,' he commented, 'appear un — ' But then he peered more closely, and a worried grunt escaped him; and after that he first lowered an ear to the plate and then sniffed at it, a bilious hue that betrayed his sudden fear creeping in under the light tan of his skin. 'You are right,' he said tauntly. 'I can smell acid. Yes, a time fuse would have been upset by the different dimension through which we are now travelling.'

'If there is an acid fuse in there,' Fisher rejoined, 'and you can smell it, the charge must be close to detonating.'

'There's no hope of smothering it,' Arle said through his teeth. 'If the explosive in use is asmaphades, there will be enough of it in the bottom of the cage to blow the ship in two. We must get rid of the cage totally — discharge it into space.'

'How in heaven's name can we do that?' Fisher asked.

'We must blow it out through a lifeboat escape tube,' Arle replied, already on his way to the door with the cage suspended from his right hand.

'The bird!' Varinia pleaded. 'Open the cage — free it!'

'I dare not!' Arle answered, disappearing into the passage outside. 'There could be a second firing device attached to the door!'

Fisher dived out of the cabin in the Lexian's wake. He made a right turn and lunged after Arle's retreating figure. The old man turned left at the end of the passage. Fisher cornered an instant later and kept on his heels. They raced across the beam of the ship, then Arle cornered again — to the right this time — and Fisher felt some relief in the others obvious knowledge of the vessel.

Arle came to a chamber that was built against the craft's hull. He charged the door open with his left shoulder and passed inside. Fisher entered immediately in the Lexian's wake, then stopped a pace or two beyond the threshold as he saw Arle come to a halt before a massive panel in which three tubes that were each about forty eight inches in diameter yawned into the room, their caps standing open on hinges. Arle shoved the birdcage into the middle tube, slammed and secured its cap, then moved to a control board adjacent, where he pulled down a handle and caused the needles on two gauges to jump abruptly as compressed air went driving out through the tube, the whole effect being similar to the firing of a torpedo from a submarine. Then, hardly more than a second later, there was a terrific detonation in the vicinity of the spaceship, and the vessel wavered momentarily in its course before hurtling onwards in the same smooth manner as before.

Arle turned away from the tubes. He

looked a much aged man as he tottered limply towards the middle of the floor, where he weakly brushed away the support that Fisher offered and said: 'As well that I remembered the tube drill from the days when, as a young man, I bucketed around the universe in one of these ships. Two seconds more would have seen the end of all of us.'

'You can hardly get closer than that,' Fisher agreed, listening to the commotion which was now audible higher in the spaceship and clearly had to do with those in charge trying to find out where the explosion had occurred. He kept track of the fluctuating approach of the voices and running footfalls, and, as he waited for Arle to show signs of returning strength, also took in the stacked presence around the room of many perspex-lidded coffin-shapes — the ship's lifeboats or survival capsules, he imagined — and was further unnerved by the sight.

Then Arle murmured: 'Come.'

They left the chamber, the Lexian walking with steps that were firm but too mechanical, and they had progressed a little way down the passage outside, when a group of uniformed men came running up, the youngish man whom Fisher had earlier identified as the captain moving in the lead. Halting, his arms outflung to stop the onrush of the six figures at his back, the commanding officer threw an anxious glance at Arle and fired off a couple of questions. He was answered with a conciseness and quiet dignity which had a generally calming effect, and the expression on his face was one of extreme gravity dissolving into relief, when Arle tried to take one pace more and crumpled to the floor at his feet.

Fisher bent to give assistance, but a fending gesture from the captain made it clear that nothing was expected or required of him; so he stepped aside and watched while Arle was first turned on to his back and then briefly examined by one of the men in the captain's company — this resulting in another man being sent off at the run, apparently to fetch a doctor; and after that, as the old man was picked up by two more of the crewmen and carried back in the direction of his cabin, he attached himself to the captain and the rest and brought up the rear.

Varinia was waiting in the passage which served the three cabins which had been allocated to the passengers. Fisher saw her throw her hands to her mouth as she beheld her father's shape between the carrying crewmen. Then, visibly pulling herself together, she opened the door of Arle's cabin for the oncoming men and stepped back, her features expressionless.

The two crewmen bore Arle into his quarters and placed him on his bunk. The captain went in behind them, ordering everybody else to remain outside in the passage. Then a man carrying a leather bag shouldered into the narrow space among them, and he was instantly given room to go on through into the cabin. Fisher had no doubt that he was the medico for whom the runner had been sent.

'What happened, Craig?' Varinia asked.

Fisher told her what had occurred, patting her shoulder as she showed traces of distress.

'Oh, Doctor Samerle!' she exclaimed

bitterly. 'To think that I was foolish enough to bring the birdcage aboard!'

'You can't blame yourself for that,' Fisher retorted. 'It isn't easy to mistrust a friend.'

'Friend?' she whispered. 'This has made me wonder how many friends we truly have.'

'Samerle is *that* important?' Fisher asked perceptively.

'More important than Khaka in the real sense,' she replied. 'His work as the scientific director places him in regular contact with everybody who matters in New Lexia, and he is also very active socially.'

'That makes the situation back there all the blacker,' Fisher admitted, seeking a grain of comfort but finding none.

A minute or so after that the captain and the two crewmen came out of the cabin door. The captain dismissed all the uniformed men present, then spoke to Varinia, who turned from him and stepped into the cabin, heading for the bunk and the man who was still active beside it.

Fisher watched from the door. He saw the doctor complete his examination of the unconscious Arle and put his stethescope away. Varinia began asking the man questions, and was courteously answered; and her worry, evident at first, grew less as the talk went on; and by the time that it had reached its end and the doctor had moved away from her, she had a smile for both him and the captain when they took their leave from the threshold and began walking back to their duties in the ship.

'What's the matter with your father?' Fisher asked.

The woman gestured for him to enter the cabin, then crossed the floor and shut the door at his back. 'The physician thinks that he has had a slight cerebral haemorrhage,' she answered. 'But he says there is no trace of paralysis, and he does not think it will develop. My father should make a complete recovery in a fairly short time.'

'If he does not recover sufficiently to take charge,' Fisher said stonily, 'you're going to have to take his place, Varinia.'

160

'I!' the woman exclaimed aghast. 'I could not possibly do that. Where's the need?'

'Consider our return to Earth,' Fisher answered. 'Doctor Samerle's guilt has been exposed. He and the other guilty — in whatever number they may be — will come at us in force if we can't show them a greater force. You must tell the authorities on Lexia all that you know concerning the murder attempts on me, then ask them for their help against the men who so obviously want to subjugate Earth rather than request her asylum. If Samerle is allowed to go unchecked, he could end up, after the spaceships have discharged their immigrants in New Lexia, as the dominant force among your people on Earth. As the power and experience already there, he could impose his will on better men until his was the only will around.'

'I follow your reasoning,' Varinia admitted. 'It is not a woman's place to take this matter up, but I will if I have to.' A mirthless chuckle escaped her, and dry bones of disillusionment rattling in it.

'Always, at the last, we are made to examine our hearts. With all that has happened to us so far, I might be tempted to let matters run their course — if I thought that New Lexia could win. But the truth my mind saw before is now as cold and real to me as if it had already happened. One lost battle on Earth could write finish to the old, old history of my people, and that I am not prepared to risk.' Her chuckle came again, lower this time. 'You win, Craig Fisher. The Lexians are not such a moral race — and I am not such a moral person.'

'I'm looking for no victories of that kind!' Fisher snorted. 'Events have advanced too far for that. So long as you are prepared to act with commonsense, I'm prepared to play my part.'

'Leave me now,' she said, her chin jerking. 'I want to be alone with my father.'

'Very well,' Fisher said, moving to the door. 'Try not to worry too much. Let's wait and see how things look at journey's end.'

He withdrew from Arle's cabin, and it

was only as he walked down the passage and re-entered his own cabin that he realized that he had been in his stockinged feet throughout all the recent activities. Then, shutting his door and dusting off his soles, he went back to his bunk and lay down again, his worry over Arle's condition and the matters that he had just discussed with Varinia occupying most of his mind, but gradually his brain grew less active and he began to doze, this restful state persisting for what seemed a very long time and only ending when a loud click from the wall at the further end of the cabin caused him to lift sharply on his left elbow and blink open his eyes.

He saw that the video screen in the wall was now alive. The picture glowing in it was that of a greenish-blue, cloud-veiled globe that was hurtling in from the deeps of the void and growing in detail through ever-enlarging frames of focus. Plainly, he was being invited to a view of the planet Lexia across the bend of the universe, but the picture also implied that the journey across space was moving towards its end.

Climbing out of his bunk, Fisher put

on his shoes and went to his chair. There he sat down and resumed watching the screen. Larger and larger grew the globe, its colours filling the cabin with an eye-aching brightness, and then the encircling gloom of space was lost and the planet filled the whole screen, its cloud shredding into a first view of land masses that were largely brown.

Still the detail magnified. There were ranges of mountains and there were rivers and plains, and there were likewise vast margins of brownish-red discolouration near the unnatural fluctuations in the tidal boundaries of the oceans that were hard to explain at first; but then it came to Fisher that they were incredibly extensive troughs and mudflats from which the seas had drained in process of a multi-continental inundation which was slowly licking the planet round. And then, as the ship moved closer yet to Lexia, he made out titanic fields of flame which were belching from zig-zag fissures that had to be hundreds of miles long, and he traced films of smoke and fumes that hovered like weeping stormbelts across the length and breadth of the spectrum. Even from this distance out in the void it was possible to see that Lexia was a world nearing the ultimate throes of self-destruction, and it seemed to Fisher that he could feel the anguished resignation of countless souls rising about him in a voiceless prayer to have done.

Once more there was that moment in which reality became tenuous and changed. The sense of plunging at a speed beyond that of thought retreated to the velocities of more common experience. Now immensity splurged into immensity, and trans-global detail was lost in the build up of local conformations on the land mass that was still least touched by the encroachment of the seas. As the spaceship headed towards the right-hand edge of this mass, blasted valleys became visible in all their scorched horror, shattered mountains gaped and belched, sulphurous clouds from the world's heart wreathed and swirled amidst towering thermals, and the lightenings of an endless tempest forked through the scudding fogs and monsoonal mudstorms that enveloped the dank lagoons and oozing deserts which Lexia's axial shift had everywhere produced.

A once fine plain spread broadly towards the finality of a landing place. This was overlooked by a towering mountain whose lately snowclad peak now thrust black and naked into the highest levels of the volcanic murk. There was a ruined city in sight of the mountain. It, too, had been splendid, and not so very long ago; for the often-washed steel which its wreckage raised in twisted majesty to the glowering light of an arching rainbow was still bright and clean, the towers of crystal and toughened glass had not wholly fragmented from the seismic shocks which had opened gulfs and canyons across the finest districts of the place, and as yet unbroken windows still created instants of ruby-like radiance amidst the slow, soggy fires of a central magnificence that had split into palatial ruin but not crumbled. Then the superb vision of soot-coated, many-fanged splendour slid mistily off the viewing screen and gave full coverage to the landing field itself.

Here, occasionally riven but mostly undamaged — since it appeared to be founded on the great mountain's apron-rock — was a concrete set down area that was several square miles in extent. On the left-hand side of it and shading towards the centre, scores of spaceships were visible, and each one of them looked even bigger than that in which Fisher was travelling. This, then, must be the fleet of spacecraft which was to carry Lexia's élite to Earth when the ultimate exodus began. So many people, so many ships; and yet, as Arle had said, the entire operation paled out of magnitude when you considered the overwhelming size of the disaster that had begotten it and the numbers who must perish for all its saviour role.

Satisfied that his own craft was within minutes of touchdown, Fisher decided that he had better go and see how Arle and Varinia were getting on. As he left his cabin, he had few hopes of finding the old man conscious, and it came to him therefore as a surprise when, at the tap of his knuckle, Arle's door opened under Varinia's hand and he saw the Project Chief from New Lexia standing beside his bunk and looking rather groggy and distrait but otherwise pretty much himself.

'Come in,' Varinia said.

He entered, exchanging relieved glances with the woman. 'How do you feel, sir?' he inquired.

Arle shrugged. 'My body is wearing up. That I cannot conceal from myself or anybody else. I can only hope that it will last long enough to enable me to complete the work that has to be done.'

Fisher nodded. The old man's summing up of his own condition was too positive to admit of reassurances or soothing contradictions. 'I was afraid we were to lack the benefit of your presence,' he admitted.

'That is not to be wondered at,' Arle said acidly. 'Samerle is no opponent for the likes of you and my daughter.'

'In this company,' Fisher acknowledged, 'I'm the alien. I have no say.'

Arle's sudden smile could only be

described as secret and slightly evil. 'On Lexia,' he agreed, 'your role will be a passive one.'

Doubts and unease possessed Fisher again. 'You never did answer the question I asked you just before we came aboard.'

'I recall no question.'

'What's your true reason for bringing me to Lexia?'

'Ah, yes,' Arle said indifferently. 'You do not believe in that intermediary business any more.'

'I haven't fully believed in it for a long time — if I ever did,' Fisher retorted. 'Can't you now tell me what my real importance to you is?'

'Time enough,' Arle advised, making no denials.

Varinia looked startled. 'But — '

'You need not concern yourself with it, daughter,' Arle interrupted.

'Need not — !'

This time she was interrupted by Fisher's warning glance. It would be most unwise to involve a man who was thought to have recently sustained a slight stroke in the kind of quarrel that looked to be brewing. Whatever the duplicity in which Arle was involved where he, Fisher, was concerned, it was better that the Project Chief should go mentally untaxed and later play his vital part in whatever had to happen on Lexia than that there should be any risk of his brain lesion being reopened during a fierce argument and his death or total incapacitation coming out of it.

Varinia subsided and turned away. There was a fraught silence in the cabin. Then Fisher felt a jolt go shuddering through the spaceship and knew that it had landed. Shortly after that there was a knock on the door and Varinia admitted the captain and the doctor. The latter had something angry to say at the sight of Arle standing before him, but the old man gestured dismissively at the words, and the doctor could only shake his head and sigh off into silence. Then, looking uncomfortable, the captain spoke and nodded towards the door; and after that he bowed and withdrew, gently pushing the medical man out into the passage ahead of him. The footfalls of the two men quickly receded.

Then Varinia turned to Fisher and said: 'We are to disembark at once. Trugel Missenheim has a car waiting for us.'

'Who's Trugel Missenheim?' Fisher asked.

'The Prime Minister of Lexia,' Arle put in, moving a trifle shakily through the door, 'and my best friend.'

Fisher and the woman followed the old man into the passage, and he led them in the direction of the hatch by which they had originally entered the spaceship. They had turned a corner or two and the door was visible ahead of them, when Fisher said: 'I saw a city on the tele-viewer in my cabin. Are we going there, sir?'

'That was Kredabah, our capital,' Arle replied. 'No, we are not going there. The captain has just told us that life in the capital is now almost impossible. We are going to Mount Purna. It seems that the Emperor and all the major government figures have removed there and are living in the chambers and galleries that have been cut within it. The mountain is formed of valorite, a rock that is many times harder than any stone on your planet and may yet survive the worst earthquakes of the last cataclysm without splitting.'

They had reached the hatch. Arle stepped through it on to the platform of an elevator which resembled the one by which they had embarked on Earth. Fisher and Varinia joined him, the former at once conscious of the foetid, storm-charged airs about them, and then the elevator began to descend, and a minute later it delivered them to what was obviously the right-hand — or eastern — fringe of the concrete spaceport which had appeared on the viewing screen, where an exceptionally tall, high-shouldered man, with sunken lineaments and wrinkling neck, came forward to meet them, a chauffeur-driven electric car of luxurious design and proportions visible at his back.

Arle and the tall man embraced like long-lost brothers. Then the former introduced his daughter, who curtsied and looked suitably shy as the towering figure squeezed her hands, and after that Arle waved casually to his left and said in

English: 'Allow me to introduce Craig Fisher, Prime Minister.'

'Mr. Fisher,' Missenheim said, his response in the Earthman's tongue suggesting that here, as in New Lexia, it was necessary for the most senior people to learn English. 'I have been looking forward to meeting you.' He offered a hand that enclosed the fingers which Fisher placed in it with a steely grip, and this held while his silvery eyes appraised the other carefully. Then, as he released his clasp, he slanted his gaze at Arle and said: 'Perfect.'

'I think so,' Arle agreed.

'How I wish we could reward you adequately, my dear old friend,' Missenheim said.

'To have served is reward enough,' Arle returned. 'How is Tuga Halshafar?'

'The Emperor is sad.'

'Naturally.'

'How long?'

'Who can be exactly sure? We hope for a week or two more; but the end could come at any time.'

'Have the seismologists made up their

minds what form it will take?'

'They are certain now that the planet's shell will hold, Arle. But the final convulsions will pitch the world westwards into a year of hurricanes and cyclic flooding that will undoubtedly wipe all but a trace or two of life from Lexia's surface.'

'That corresponds with the last information beamed to Earth,' Arle observed, 'and is much what I expected to hear. Do you know, aware that it could not be, I yet went down on my knees and prayed for a reprieve?'

'We have all prayed,' Missenheim said. 'You have come back to a world that believes only in Divine Wrath.'

'Well,' Arle commented, 'if we cannot hope for Divine Aid, we can at least hope that the luck which we have enjoyed so far will last that short time more. If we can get our future settled on Earth, before the exodus is forced on us, the migrants should not suffer unduly. Should it happen otherwise, there could be difficulty; for the resources of New Lexia are not inexhaustible, and they would soon be under strain from the presence of more than three hundred thousand people.'

'We realize that,' Missenheim said. 'How does Mr. Fisher think his world will react to our request for living space?'

'The iron fist in our velvet glove troubles him.'

'Not surprisingly.'

'Doctor Samerle and his warmongers trouble me even more,' Fisher declared.

'What's that about Samerle?' Missenheim demanded of Arle.

'Something that Mr. Fisher is tending to over-emphasize, Prime Minister. A domestic problem mainly. I will deal with it when I get back to Earth.'

'Nevertheless,' Missenheim said, 'I must insist on hearing about it. You and I can discuss it as we travel on to Mount Purna. Into the car with the three of you.'

The cover of Missenheim's vehicle was already raised. Fisher and Varinia stepped into the back of the car, while Arle and the Prime Minister seated themselves behind the driver, who then pulled the cover down and moved off, turning almost at once into an exit road on the right and shortly after that picking up a highway which gave access to the lower slopes of the mountain which now soared into full view before them.

Heads bent together, Arle and Missenheim talked, and Fisher heard Samerle's name mentioned several times. He rather thought that the Prime Minister would want to question him, and waited expectantly, but presently the two old friends relaxed and began to jabber like a pair of youngsters, and he knew that they had threshed out the Samerle matter without recourse to him and relaxed also.

By now they were well on to the mountain. The road staggered into long zigs and zags. The car's power unit shrilled a little on the steepest of the grades, but progress was steady and the altitude increased. Fisher peered back and down. To the south he saw the ruins of Kredabah under their canopy of flying soot and smoke, while to the west he again saw the full spread of the spaceport and its distant fleet of interstellar transports. Straying east, his eye caught the isolated spacecraft that had recently come in from Earth, and he suffered a pang of homesickness. He tried an inward laugh at the idea that it might be prophetic. For home seemed like a place that he might never see again.

He looked to the front once more. Another thought that had Earth associations came. This was just like the climb up to the auto tunnel on the Italian side of Mt. Blanc — especially as he could now discern a tunnel mouth at the foot of the grey and metallic cliffs that stood above the staggered sections of the highway on the lower slopes.

The car whined upwards for another five minutes, and the end of the ascent drew near. They passed a guard point, and the armed men standing about it saluted the Prime Minister's car. Then the tunnel yawned before them, its polished bore reaching back into the mountainside and carrying with it the silver glitter of linked bulbs amidst damp shadows.

Slowing down, the driver entered the rock. For the next two hundred yards the car followed the slight left-hand bend of the passage. Then all parallel between the tunnels on Mt. Blanc and Purna ended, for the present passage suddenly lost its identity in a large and brightly lighted chamber out of which several other tunnels radiated. The driver crossed into one of these that opened more-or-less opposite that by which they had entered, and after that they went a considerable distance further before coming to a stop in a bottle-shaped room that held a number of other vehicles and had the appearance of a garage.

The chauffeur raised the car's top. Then he got out and assisted the Prime Minister and Arle to alight. After that he offered Varinia a hand, but left Fisher to step out of the vehicle unaided. Next, while Missenheim and company waited, the man went to a shelf nearby and picked up a phone that was located there. He spoke into it, questioning, and appeared to receive an answer in the affirmative, after which he gestured respectfully that the party could go on, and the Prime Minister led his three companions to the top end of the garage, where they entered a short passage that gave into a well and then ascended a spiral staircase, coming out on a rock landing at the summit of the climb.

Here they were met by an armed man. He looked them over, bowing to the Prime Minister, then turned to some machinery that was in evidence against the wall on his right. He pulled a lever, and, as the bar slid down the slot that had been cut for it in the stone, a door rumbled upwards in the rockface adjacent, thus revealing the entrance to a chamber which had gone totally unsuspected by the watching Fisher until then.

Beckoning for the trio from Earth to follow, Missenheim entered the secret room. Arle and Varinia passed in behind the Prime Minister, and Fisher stepped through at their backs, his nostrils twitching to the sweet and holy smell of incense. Then, under lights which beamed down from the roof about twenty feet above, Fisher saw that he was in a place of some magnificence, for there were rich tapestries around the wall, the floor was deeply rugged, and the furniture standing around was of fine woods and superbly carved. Taking in the whole scene from the left, his eyes came finally to rest on a bay that had been cut into the wall on the right. This, too, was tastefully adorned with brocades and other draperies, and at its centre was a dais, on top of which stood a throne of gold and many jewels. Tiny fountains splashed to left and right at the rear of the dais, and two incense burners were situated in the same positions at the front. This could only be the Emperor's throne-room, and, considering the shambles of the planet without, it appeared a very safe and comfortable one indeed.

Then Fisher detected a slight movement of the draperies at the back of the bay. Now he saw a man standing in the shadows there. The other advanced slowly; he was of better than middle height and well-proportioned; and, as he came more clearly into view, it was apparent that his hair was not of a Lexian's snowy whiteness, but dark brown — like Fisher's — and then his eyes revealed themselves as hazel-coloured, again like Fisher's, and his skin too was far paler than that common to the men of Lexia. A strange feeling creeping through his nerves, Fisher looked intently into the other's square-cut, strong-nosed, high-browed face, and he was confirmed in a familiarity that stunned him; for he was looking at himself.

But not quite it seemed, for the other said: 'I am Tuga Halshafar.'

And then Fisher understood what his true importance had been to Arle all along.

7

Fisher obeyed his first instinct and spun towards the door by which he had come in, but he saw that Trugel Missenheim had already dropped back and sealed the exit with its stone door, a challenging smile upon his face as he stood there with his hand upon a lever which was the counterpart of the one which the guard had pulled on the other side of the rock wall. 'Be sensible about this, Mr. Fisher,' he advised. 'You are fifteen light years from home, the mountain is packed with guards who can be alerted at the touch of a button, and the world beyond is in ruins. There is nowhere for you to go. If you escaped, it would be worth no more to you than days of starvation and possible infection.'

'You are going to use me to take the place of your already disguised Emperor,' Fisher accused. 'A white wig, a pair of silver contact lenses, and a slight darkening of the skin will turn me into a very good Lexian double for him. He will be able to take my place on Earth, won't he? He'll be able to meet the United Nations as Craig Fisher, and put your Lexian requests in the kind of bold and compelling language that I would never have attempted.'

'Exactly,' the Prime Minister admitted. 'I would expect our great ruler to achieve more on our behalf than Craig Fisher ever could.'

'This is — infamous!'

'Did you imagine that the élite of this planet would leave their Emperor to his death?' Missenheim demanded.

'He's a fraud and a traitor!' Fisher flung back. 'Much comfort he'll provide for his dying people. He's the rat that leaves the sinking ship!'

'You will speak with more respect!' the Emperor cut in. 'The great have great needs that are not for the little to question.'

Fisher looked Tuga Halshafar up and down, for the first time fully taking in his

London tailoring and university tie. 'You were described to me as semi-divine, Halshafar. All I can see is a hard-faced, dictatorial aristocrat who has been encouraged to believe that murder and underhandedness are ennobled when they are practised in his name.'

'I will have you executed!' the Emperor warned, shaking with fury.

'I think not,' Fisher retorted contemptuously. 'I'm far too important to your semi-divine highness for that. And to these' — he indicated Missenheim, Arle, and Varinia with a slashing gesture of his right hand — 'perpetrators of low intrigue.'

'You will not include my daughter in this!' Arle snapped. 'She knew nothing of our plot. Excluding the Emperor himself, it was in fact known only to myself, the Prime Minister, and one or two other very high officers of State.'

'I suppose you'd naturally have taken good care that no word of it could possibly reach the common people, here or on Earth,' Fisher agreed, not a whit less scathingly, though he glanced an apology at the woman. 'The millions must, at all costs, die believing themselves blessed by the Emperor's presence. Even now it would be very difficult for you if word of the truth got out. The adoration of Halshafar would cease, and the interstellar transports come under siege from the outraged common folk.' He filled his lungs to ease his bitterness. 'This plot must have been a long time in the hatching. When did it start?'

Arle and Missenheim looked uncertain as to whether they should speak or not, but the Emperor said: 'Tell him. What difference can it make? There's no help for him anywhere.'

'It began about sixteen years ago,' Arle explained. 'The Prime Minister saw the present means of saving our beloved Tuga Halshafar for the élite of his race when the day of the exodus should dawn. Trugel Missenheim summoned me from Earth and discussed it with me at his home in Kredabah. I thought his plan workable, and our first task was to pick out a young man on your planet as nearly like the Emperor as possible. Clearly, in view of the part that the Earthman would ostensibly be required to play — especially with regard to the representations that would have to be made concerning him to the British Government and the United Nations — it was necessary for him to be of high intelligence and mentally orientated to suit our Lexian character and ways. Thus we scanned the Earth from New Lexia, and were fortunate in our discovery of you, who were then in your university years.' He smiled thinly. 'But chance and destiny cover less than we suppose. Do you remember Ganymede, Mr. Fisher, the tutor at St. George's College who first turned your mind to those popular aspects of the occult which have since become of so much interest on Earth?'

'Why, yes, I recall Joseph Ganymede,' Fisher answered in a startled voice, visualising the sharp-featured, leathery, opaque-eyed Academic whose name had been brought up. 'That, too, becomes clear. He was one of you!'

'Precisely,' Arle agreed. 'Not only did Ganymede guide you by day, but he also used mechanical feed devices to influence your mind while you slept. To a large extent, you are our creation; the man of slight prominence — Craig Fisher, author — whom we needed for a plan which we gambled at the beginning would not take us beyond the present time.'

Fisher felt his shoulders sag. It wasn't so much that he felt stunned as humiliated. So little that he had achieved had been his own. Throughout his adult life, then, the mill of his subconscious had been churning out a product that was essentially somebody else's. His creativity had been a conditioned reflex, and the high-toned knowledge that he had dispensed had been the means to another's end. And what had it all been about. This!

'Knowing what you now know,' the Prime Minister said shrewdly, 'don't you feel that we have some right to make use of you? We gave you the odd hour of acclaim, we gave you fulfilment; we charged your mediocrity with inspiration. The work you did will remain. It has solid value, and will honour your name. Accept your fate here as payment for a service rendered.' He took Fisher by the shoulders and gave him what affected to be a friendly and encouraging shake. 'You have spoken of murder. There could only be murder intended here if there were a guarantee of your death. You may survive the last cataclysm, and others may survive it with you. These galleries are ten thousand feet above sea level, and the rock is unlikely to split. More. There are almost unlimited supplies of all kinds in the storerooms, and the generators — unless submerged by the rising tide — will be running a hundred years from now. When the Emperor and we, his servants, have departed, you will need only to sit on the throne and face the television camera which covers it from the wall opposite, so that those still surviving around Lexia will be able to see pictures of you and take heart — this at such times as a loyal one who shall be left with you will indicate — and the remainder of the hours will be yours for the enjoyment of the ample comforts of this place. Come now, Mr. Fisher! You have always been an idealist. Would you deny our dying millions the comfort of your smile? There is nothing for it but to co-operate when there is nothing else to do. We go forth to a life of striving. You may yet turn out to have been the lucky one.'

'It could be so,' Fisher returned, his spirit rising again in a defiance that was the more savage for his previous hurt. 'The masters of Lexia may not find themselves the masters of New Lexia. Arle, you still have Doctor Samerle and his unknown warmongers to put down before you can get on with gammoning the United Nations.'

'What is this?' the Emperor demanded.

'A small matter in New Lexia, sire, that I can easily put right,' Arle replied.

'I will not be fobbed off!' the Emperor declared.

'There is dissension in New Lexia,' Missenheim cut in to explain. 'Arle has spoken to me of it. There are those under his authority who would rather undertake the subjugation of Earth than make requests of its leaders.'

'Oh, that,' Tuga Halshafar said dismissively. 'I have seen enough of this place.

Let us go to the spaceport.'

'The haste might appear unseemly, sire,' the Prime Minister warned. 'The spaceship from Earth has not been led to expect so swift a turn round.'

'How is my disguise, Prime Minister?'

'Faultless, sire,' Missenheim assured him.

'And my English?'

'Perfect.'

'Then to any or all whom it may concern,' the Emperor said decisively, 'I am Craig Fisher. He came, he spoke with the appropriate people, and now he goes.' He smiled craftily at his Prime Minister. 'Will it not be easier to neutralise this Samerle faction if my true identity remains concealed for as long as possible?'

'If you put it like that, sire,' Missenheim said — 'yes, it would.'

'Then have no fear that anybody here or on Earth will know me — before I choose — for other than the man whom I purport to be.' Tuga Halshafar preened himself openly. 'Have I not spent years studying Craig Fisher in all his facets? You may have faith in the voice recordings and video films with which you equipped me.'

'We have faith in you, sire,' the Prime Minister assured him.

'Then open the door.'

Missenheim turned to the lever and depressed it. The hidden door opened almost silently in the wall. The Emperor strode by the Earthman and passed through the exit. Fisher gazed after the ruler, knowing that the facts that he had been given of what escape would mean were true ones; but, feeling all the same that any kind of freedom — or even death — would be preferable to being the dupe of the Lexian leaders, he decided to dive for the doorway as Missenheim, Arle, and Varinia made to pass through it. He hoped that he would be able to get away in the resulting confusion of bodies, but had no more than set himself for the plunge, when fingers settled on a nerve centre at the base of his neck and began to apply pressure with great strength. It occurred to him that another person must have entered the throne-room through that opening at the back of the dais from which Halshafar had first appeared, and, as he felt paralysis setting in and his consciousness ebbing, he tried to twist his head round and catch a glimpse of the newcomer — who could only be that 'loyal one' of whom the Prime Minister had spoken — but the darkness closed about him before he could make out a single feature, and he fell towards the floor.

His brain was fuzzy for several moments after he had regained his senses, but his memory itself was clear enough, and, as he felt the comfort of a bed beneath him and his nostrils twitched to the smell of incense again, he wondered once more about the identity of his attacker and opened his eyes at the same slow and unprovoking rate as he sat up, his gaze roving mistily around the rock chamber of fair dimensions that had a mirror, clothes rails, and screened off toilet facilities, and had in fact been furnished as a bedroom — if you discounted the huge video screen which stared dully out of the wall on the right and accepted a claustrophobic stuffiness which the air-conditioning did not seem fully able to deal with.

Then Fisher saw the person he sought: the one who logically had to be there. The other was sitting on a stool that was situated between the foot of the divan bed and a door which was covered on the outside by a brocade curtain which Fisher recognised as part of the drapery that covered the walls of the bay in which the throne-room dais was set. The Lexian was a human nightmare. Altogether gigantic, he was hideously deformed, his back being hunched and his head placed too close to it. Worse, his ears protruded like cabbage leaves, his nose was a squashed bulb of a venomous redness, and his jagged teeth either lay back in his pale gums or added a touch of jutting rottenness to a grin that could as well have been a scowl amidst so much disfigurement. 'Who are you?' Fisher asked, hardly expecting an answer, yet even more surprised by the revelation that followed.

Opening his mouth wide, the other made a clucking noise which revealed that he had only the stump of a tongue, and then he clapped his hands over his ears, unmistakably to make it plain that he was deaf. 'Deaf and dumb,' Fisher commented. 'Your kind do indeed make the best and most loyal of servants. I think I'll call you Quasimodo. It's the only name I can think of that suits.'

Fisher slid off the side of the bed and stood up. Fingering the tender spot on the base of his neck where the nerve centre had been depressed, he started a trifle unsteadily for the door, more than half-expecting the other to rise and interpose himself, but Quasimodo made no move of any kind and Fisher reached the curtained exit a moment or two later. Drawing aside the brocade drape, he looked out into the throne-room, the dais intruding on much of his view, and then stepped through the door and rounded the raised structure on its left, his tread growing faster and faster as he made for the hidden door by which he had first entered the Emperor's rooms. He found himself running over the last part of the floor, and he was breathless and dizzy when he reached the lever that controlled the opening and shutting of the rock door, though he still had strength enough to push it down and wait for the aperture to appear before him; but nothing happened and the wall remained fast closed.

After that he worked the lever up and down many times, desperation giving way to anger and anger turning back into desperation, but still he had no luck; and, stepping back at last, he was forced to accept what he had known to be the case from the first: the machinery which operated the door had been immobilised from the outside — doubtless at the time that the Emperor, Missenheim, Arle, and Varinia had left — and he and the crippled Lexian were total prisoners in the mountain's core. Small wonder the Quasimodo had made no effort to forestall his movements in here.

Turning away from the lever, Fisher walked slowly back in the direction from which he had come, stopping at the middle of the throne-room floor to look down at the change of garments which he had just realized that he had been given. His garb was now that of a high caste Lexian, the trousers spotless and the knee-length robe without a crease. Then, a slight discomfort to his eyeballs causing him to fear worse still, he hurried back into the bedchamber, where he went to the mirror and saw reflected what he had become resigned to seeing — the silvery eyes and snow white hair of a counterfeit Lexian who did indeed look very much as he imagined that Tuga Halshafar must look in his normal form.

He pulled at his head, expecting to find that it was topped by a wig, but the hair held fast and the tug at its roots informed him that it had been dyed to suit the rest of his make-up. Irritated, he lowered his hands to his eyes and prepared to find relief for the latest frustration by taking out the contact lenses which were hiding his brown pupils, but the still seated Quasimodo rose at this and made a threatening gesture; so, as he saw nothing to be gained from totally polarising his enforced relationship with the muscular cripple, he dropped his hands to his sides and shrugged, turning from the mirror and starting to pace up and down, the appalling fact of his imprisonment and its purpose weighing on his spirit as only an irreversible fact possibly could.

Then a new reason for disquiet impinged on his troubled mind. First rasping and distant, then crashing and rolling into near reverberations out of which came a quaking that seemed to rock the mountain itself, the tremors of a major earthquake manifested. Coming to a standstill near the wall behind his bed, Fisher clenched his fists and sweated, for he felt like a microscopic life form in the grip of forces that overwhelmed the imagination. The disturbance continued. For the Earthman one minute followed the next in dragging, nerve-fraying uncertainty as to whether the end was near; but the cripple accepted it all with the calm of one who had experienced it all before, and the trembling was past its worst when he walked to the video screen on his left and pressed the first of a line of switches beneath it, bringing in a picture of seas that undulated ominously under

197

the blackest of clouds and horizons where the tidal forces raised by the earthquake were already pressing and bursting in white torrents that would shortly hit the land with new floods that would submerge further tracts of country which, from the evidence of contour and dead vegetation, had once been far from the ocean shore.

Fisher would have given much to have been able to talk with his deaf-and-dumb keeper. It would have been a blessing could he have asked how far the waters were from Mount Purna, and where the camera was placed from which the present picture was coming; how much fresh harm each new disturbance brought, and how many people died by fire and flood and subsidence each day: and other questions relevant and otherwise; but he could only go on watching silently as Quasimodo rumbled in his chest and brought in other pictures, the sequence presenting vistas of fire and doom and unrelieved destruction that plainly encompassed the planet round. Then, as the last of the tremors grumbled away into stilly silence, Fisher forced himself to assimilate what he had seen in a spirit of clinical detachment. The destruction out there was really too stupendous to view in any kind of personalized way. Planetary death was almost an accomplished fact. One man's hope of survival — and even his fear — seemed almost blasphemous in the face of that.

Fisher resumed his restless pacing. Despite his conscious efforts to reduce tension in himself, he felt an anticipatory tightness that would not go away. He knew by instinct that the district's next bout of shaking could not be long delayed. Yet there was also boredom in his uneasiness, and he sought relief from that boredom — without expecting to find any; but then his questing eyes made out a low cupboard behind the clothes rails which he had not spotted before, and he sidled through to it and opened the double doors at its front, finding in it a reproducer and a variety of tapes.

Removing the machine from the cupboard, he carried it to the bed, and had discovered how it worked and was about to play one of the tapes, when he felt a peremptory tap on the back and then a hand turning him towards the throne-room door. Fisher took it that he was required to make his first telecast as the substitute Tuga Halshafar, and his resentment stirred at the compulsion that was present, but he reminded himself of the need to avoid senseless friction with the giant cripple, and was also aware of the specious moral obligation that Missenheim had placed on him. If those who still survived on Lexia could find their brainwashed comfort in looking at his face, then he supposed that he had better provide a willing service. He certainly had nothing better to do, and there had to be some satisfaction in helping the doomed to meet their ends stoically. To start issuing irate declamations in English — which might well give the audience the impression that the semi-divine Emperor was cracking under the strain — would unquestionably be counter-productive.

Guided by Quasimodo, Fisher re-entered the throne-room and allowed himself to be escorted up the steps of the dais. He sat down on the throne — which was a far from comfortable seat — and looked towards the aperture in the wall opposite through which he could see the lense of a television camera pointing at him. Apparently satisfied by his co-operation, the giant cripple withdrew down the steps and retreated audibly towards the room from which he and his charge had just emerged. Rising slightly in his seat, Fisher craned after the departed man, and it was then he discovered that Quasimodo's trust was not as childlike as it seemed, for the thinnest of steel bands suddenly shot out and locked his wrists to the arms of the throne and his ankles to its legs. Grimacing, he settled again; there would at least be no possibility of his becoming camera shy; and then he saw a red transmission light start burning near the lense which was pointing at him, and he lapsed into remotely smiling contemplation of the countless faces that he could not see.

The red light burned for about an hour; then it went out. Assuming both the telecast and his first period of duty at an end, Fisher pulled experimentally at his arms and legs, and the steel bands jumped back into their hidden slots and left him free again, suggesting that the locks worked in conjunction with the switch of the camera itself and whatever programming had been projected against his enforced occupation of the throne. Here was another example of how cold-bloodedly his Lexian users had planned to deceive and exploit him, and he was in no mood to make an agreeable response when he stepped back into the bedchamber a few moments later and received a look from the giant cripple which seemed to say: 'There, that wasn't so bad, was it?'

He sat down with the reproducer again, and after that — still breathlessly sensitive to the faintest quiver in his environment — spent an hour or two playing over about a dozen tapes. Most of the recordings were of music, and much of this was strangely orchestrated and not very beautiful to the Earth-conditioned ear, but two of the tapes were of English lessons that had been largely Earth-recorded, and it was strange and yet comforting to hear snippets from B.B.C.

news bulletins, fragments of conversation eavesdropped in Earthly streets, orders shouted on bridge and parade ground, and spoutings from the amateur stage. These lessons were undoubtedly part of the course from which the Emperor had learned his English, and, as Fisher listened to the teacher's interjections and explanations of grammar and syntax in the Lexian tongue, he realized how far the two languages were apart and thought it unlikely that he could have imitated his exploiters' feat of learning had their situations been reversed.

Then, from some concealed pantry about the place, the giant cripple produced a meal of bread and fruit and wine; and, while they were eating it — and Fisher was asking himself how many other points of concealment there might be in the apparently unbreached walls around him — another earthquake came. This one more than matched the severity of the one that had gone before, and when, hard on its heels, another of still greater force manifested, Quasimodo showed his first trace of agitation and hurried to the video screen, switching to the first seascape that he had shown and peering intently at waves of preternatural immensity that were now flooding towards a strand that had lately receded to within a few degrees of the recording camera's deepest angle of scan. Taking this view as the one to which the huge freak was most sensitive, the process of inundation could well have speeded to the extent that Quasimodo believed the Mount Purna area to be in fairly imminent danger of drowning.

At last the tremors ceased again, and Fisher found himself — not unexpectedly — hurried into the throne-room once more, where he mounted the dais and seated himself a second time, the thin steel bands again securing his limbs to the arms and legs of the throne as the latest telecast began.

Again the red light opposite burned for about an hour. On this occasion, however, Fisher found watching the camera a trifle less endurable, and he resorted to all kinds of mental exercises to reduce the ennui of the period. But at last the bracelets released him again, and left him free to rise — which he did for as long as was necesary to stretch the stiffened joints of his elbows and knees — and then he sat down once more and matched the soreness of his backside to the hardness of the throne, for he had no desire to rejoin Quasimodo in the bed-chamber and was beginning to feel that he might just as well wait in his present seat from one telecast to the next as sit on the bed yonder and contemplate the further horrors of the video screen.

Then, after he had been sitting there a few minutes more, a tremendous detonation of a gaseous nature seemed to occur under the mountain itself and he felt the countless millions on tons of valorite of which Purna was formed start to settle and shake in a manner which caused the lights to begin blinking off and on and the walls to bend and scream about him to the extent that the collapse of the chamber seemed inevitable; yet somehow the toughness of the valorite survived the apex of the distubance, and after that the shock waves diminished and the mountain resumed much of its original solidity of stance.

For a time the echoes went on; but then the silence returned and the lights resumed their steady beaming. The stillness became profound; that of the grave had nothing on it. But the renewed sense of waiting in the portentous hush was terrifying, and Fisher was filled by a vast loneliness of the flesh and spirit. Suddenly he could stand it no more, and did the one thing that he had not dreamed he would do — fled off the dais and back into the Emperor's sleeping place, sheerly to regain the company of his hideous keeper, who was still watching the video screen and the tumultuous foaming of the seas, which had now entirely blotted out the land contours which he had seen not much more than four hours ago and which now seemed to be climbing steadily towards the position occupied by the camera which was taking the incoming picture.

Fisher lay down on the bed now. For a little while he watched the screen almost despite himself, and then he ceased looking at it and turned over. The desolation had changed into fatigue and fatalism. There was nothing he could do to alter any part of the situation; whatever must come would come. He might as well try to sleep and forget.

He found a brief oblivion; but then the mountain trembled again, and soon after that he was conducted back to the throne for another telecast. And so it went on, through dimensions of nightmare and periods of waking terror, and the time went with it; and there came at last another hour when, as the bracelets released him in his elevated seat, he decided to go on sitting in preference to rejoining Quasimodo, and Purna convulsed and the bowels of the planet thundered, but the loneliness of it troubled him no more.

Then came a surprise that jerked him clean out of his resignation. His eyes were shut when he felt a pair of arms that were young and soft around his neck. Lips kissed his with a passion that made him kiss back, and he opened his eyes on to the face of a beautiful girl. Now he made to disconnect her grip on him, but she resisted, weeping and leech-like, and he could do no more than again respond to her affection and try to comfort her, saying: 'It's all right, girl — it's all right. But where did you spring from?'

Her sobbing checked. There was a slight stiffening of her body. She drew back her face and looked at him with wet eyes in which there was a certain amount of questioning surprise.

'I suppose you are real,' Fisher said, more to himself than her now. 'I'm not hallucinating?'

The girl swallowed, then spoke, the question-mark loud at the close of her words.

'I can't understand you,' Fisher admitted.

Very puzzled by her failure to get through to him, the girl repeated herself.

'Sorry.'

She said something else, pleading, a pout to her lips and the tears starting again; then, as if comprehension came to her with the force of a blow, she reeled back to the length of her arms and stared deeply into his face, her eyes slowly widening with a disbelief that became fear; and then she let go of his neck and backed off down the steps of the dais, dodging away to her right as she reached the floor and heading for the most distant wall of the chamber, her retreat turning into a full run as Quasimodo suddenly appeared from behind the dais and went lumbering after her, his fists waving furiously in the air.

The girl reached the wall. It seemed to Fisher that the corner of a tapestry stirred, and then she disappeared. The giant cripple went right up to the spot and stood growling over it, his slow wits evidently a trifle confused by what the revelation meant to his keeper's task.

But there was no such confusion in Fisher's mind. A way out existed at the top of the room — at least into some other part of the mountain — and he intended to pass through it. If that meant he must fight Quasimodo, he was ready to try it, and he left the throne and ran down the steps of the dais, prepared to take the cripple from the rear.

However, what the deformed Lexian lacked in mental power and hearing, it was soon apparent that he made up for in instinct; for, as the oncoming Earthman jumped at him, he bent towards his toes, and, unable to check himself, Fisher drove his stomach against the cripple's buttocks and bounced off, most of the wind knocked out of him. Floundering now, he fought to recover himself, but, before he could get his hands up, Quasimodo turned and pushed him further off balance. Then, obviously not wishing to damage a face that had to be seen on television, the deformed giant let go a punch to the solar plexus, and Fisher dropped to his knees and crouched there paralysed, aware now that his escape attempt had been precipitate and ill-judged; for he ought to have left it to a later moment when his keeper was completely off guard. But it was easy to be wise after the event.

Fearing for an instant that Quasimodo was about to do him more damage, Fisher watched the other bend over him;

then the deformed man caught him under the armpits, jerked him erect, got a shoulder under his bruised middle, and then lifted him as if he weighed no more than a child. After that the giant cripple carried him back to the dais, climbed the steps, dumped him back on the throne, and finally stood over him wagging a finger and scowling what would happen if he tried it again.

Fisher nodded feebly. He was ready to admit that he was beaten for the time being, and he had no doubt that Quasimodo would always have the best of him in a fight; but the other was human and, if he hadn't slept yet, would have to sleep in the end. When that hour came — assuming that there was time left for the waiting game — Fisher promised himself that he would give the deformed man a knock on the head and then search for the secret way out and depart at his leisure. Beyond that — forgetting the girl and all that her presence had probably meant — he would be content just to wander free and unasking until the tragedy of Lexia had played itself out and he was no more. Of complications he had had enough: of striving he had had enough; all he wanted now was a last peace of mind.

But that, of course, was too much to ask for. As he glanced to the right of Quasimodo, he saw that a new phase of difficulty was beginning. The girl had reappeared from the wall, and with her was a middle-aged man who wore the white robe and trousers of Lexia's élite. And, as the crippled giant rounded on the pair with his fists raised in a new expression of fury, the man lifted a shock-pistol and sternly matched threat for threat.

8

Seeing that Quasimodo was going to charge, Fisher kicked out his right foot and tried to trip him down the side of the dais; but the deformed Lexian moved that fraction too quickly for him and thus avoided the tripping toes. He was already at the base of the steps and well-launched into his ungainly charge, when a lightning flash zipped between the man on the other side of the room and his chest. Quasimodo halted as if he had run into an immovable object; and then he spun violently and fell on his stomach.

Fisher stood up and walked down the steps of the dais. Ignoring the ache in his midriff, he bent over the giant cripple and saw at once that he was dead. Then Fisher straightened again and faced the girl and the man with the shock-pistol. They began to advance on him. The girl pointed in his direction and said something to her companion; and the other replied harshly and went on watching the Earthman with a distinctly menacing eye. 'It's difficult for you, too,' Fisher conceded, as the advancing man and the girl stopped about six feet before him. 'I can only hope, sir, that you understand me better than she does.'

'I understand you perfectly well,' came the retort. 'What has happened here? You look like the Emperor, but you are not he. Where is Tuga Halshafar?'

Rolling his eyes down, Fisher removed the contact lenses from them. 'Can't you guess?' he asked, letting the other see the colour of his pupils. 'Didn't you already know? Although you are one of those who have learned my language, am I to take it that you were not one of the privileged few?'

'I am Harbiskoom, the Lord Chamberlain,' the other replied guardedly. 'If I follow you correctly, I was not one of the privileged few. I knew that an Earthman was to be brought to Lexia for instruction in certain matters, but I didn't know that he was to stay and Tuga Halshafar to go. This switch is a barefaced deception

— the betrayal of a royal trust — the most shameful business that I have ever encountered.'

'And much else,' Fisher assured him. 'Anyway, I imagine the Emperor is on Earth by now.'

'As many other Lexians will soon be,' Harbiskoom commented, looking up and about him uneasily as the chamber in which they stood rocked and rang from another sequence of volcanic explosions in the ground far beneath it. 'The ultimate catastrophe is even nearer than the most pessimistic of our scientists had previously believed, and the first ships of our exodus have already loaded up and entered space.'

'Will you help me to get home?' Fisher asked. 'Or will you compel me to play out this deception to the finish?'

'I will help you,' Harbiskoom answered grimly. 'I will see to it that you join the same spaceship on which Magina Entovitz and I myself have places. Magina' — he indicated the girl beside him — 'will be as happy as I to stand you up beside Tuga Halshafar and let our people see what a sham he has been.'

While he was reasonably confident that he could guess Magina Entovitz's place in the supposedly ascetic Emperor's life, Fisher was about to seek confirmation of it and an explanation of the girl's seemingly providential appearance in the throne-room, when the floor shook so violently that the three of them were thrown off their feet and an awful rending in the rock above their heads told that the mountain had at last sustained real injury from the earthquakes. The lights went out, and, as the toppled trio scrambled to their feet in the utter blackness, it seemed that the power had gone for good; but then the lights above flashed and flickered into life again — though giving out a most uncertain glow — and the Lord Chamberlain grabbed Fisher by the sleeve and the girl by the hand and shouted: 'Hurry! We must leave the mountain at once!'

They ran to the spot where Harbiskoom and Magina Entovitz had emerged from the wall. The Lord Chamberlain turned the obscuring tapestry aside. He shouldered against stone, and a perfectly cut door that operated on a simple swivel turned and gave access to a dimly lighted passage behind it. The Lexian entered the tunnel. Bowing their heads, Magina and Fisher followed the man through the exit. Then the three of them scuttled down the descending passage beyond, the bore shivering ahead and around them as the mountain pulsed to volcanic detonations that came with greater and greater frequency and were building up to a level of destructive vibration that even the mass of Purna could not withstand.

The tunnel walls tore and split. Gases swirled poisonously out of the cracks. The way ahead hazed into sulphurous obscurity; but, coughing and rubbing at their eyes, the escaping three continued their descent; and, mercifully, the lights still burned and showed them something of the path.

They came to a second of the swivel doors. This stood open and provided access to a rock chamber that resembled a kitchen of sorts. Here tendrils of mustard-coloured smoke wreathed in the glimmering light, their presence smudging outlines and forming a mist that scoured the throat and fouled the tongue. On the right-hand side of the room, between the plates of two cooking ranges, was an open door. Through it came fairly distant sounds of shouting and confused movement. Fisher saw Harbiskoom turn towards the noises, clearly getting ready to renew his lead in that direction; but then the lights faded in a manner which brought an intuitive warning that their approaching extinction would be final, and the Lord Chamberlain checked and turned aside, opening a cupboard out of which he took a torch.

Now Harbiskoom went out through the door on the right. Fisher and Magina Entovitz moved on to his heels again. Another tunnel descended before them, its direction taking a dexter curve in what trace of light remained, and, as he and his companions ran into the bend, Fisher had the impression that the bore was making for the big radial chamber which he had seen as the first of the mountain's major excavations. Then, before any confirmation of this could arrive, the last of the electricity failed, and in the same instant, as a response to the prolonged shaking from the ground below, there came a splintering crash as iron-hard rock showered into the passage ahead and created the kind of fall which did more than the sudden darkness to bring the running trio to a sliding stop.

Harbiskoom switched on his torch. Its ray thrust out cleanly into the blackness before them. Again the three moved ahead, but now their steps had a tentative and anxious quality; and then Fisher saw a cloud of harsh and glittering grit floating at them out of the continuing bend, and, beyond it, the roof-high presence of a rock-fall that rendered further movement to the front impossible.

Nothing was said. The Lord Chamberlain faced round, pushed between his companions, and started following his torchlight back in the direction from which they had come, Fisher and the girl instantly turning into pursuit. Shortly after that they re-entered the kitchen.

Here, too, the roof had started falling in, and they had to round piles of jagged rubble as they bowed an apprehensive course through the dust-showering threats of new falls and came to the room's farther side, where Fisher now perceived another door. Harbiskoom opened this on to an upward-trending passage that appeared to be still undamaged, but which also possessed the disadvantage of seeming to offer them no more than a way deeper into the mountain.

Once more Harbiskoom went on without hesitation. The beam of his torch probed black distance and reflected off the glassy smoothness of the machine-cut walls. The mountain cracked and reverberated, its latest falls rumbling into honeycombed places and forcing displaced airs through ducts unseen and into the faces of the climbing trio. Fear pressed at Fisher's temples, but he was hardly aware of the straining of his heart and lungs; and, judging from the gaunt and intense expressions which he saw in the brief glimpses that he received of his companions' pallid features, it was the same with them. The forces of self-preservation were now driving the three of them relentlessly.

Presently the tunnel began curving to the right, and they came to a flight of steps which moved with the turn. This they climbed, and the stair soon arrived at a landing which gave on to a second, and thereafter a repeating system of similar stairways carried them upwards under an arching roof to a final gallery which admitted the chill of the outer air and had daylight at the end of it.

The last passage terminated in a door which was shaped like the head of an arrow. They passed out of this and on to a broad, arching ledge which had been cut into the side of the mountain. The Lord Chamberlain switched off his torch and thrust it into one of the capacious pockets with which the Lexian robe was equipped. Then he and the two people with him stopped at the middle of the shelf to catch their breath.

Looking up and around, Fisher took the light to be that of the afternoon; but the sky was boiling with dark clouds and he could see nothing of Lexia's sun. He shivered in a psychic pang; the air carried a strangely robbed sense of foreboding. He moved nearer to the edge of the shelf, conscious now that they had emerged on the side of Purna opposite to that which he had entered in the Prime Minister's car and that he was facing east. Beneath him was a truly awesome gulf that was thousands of feet deep and miles across it in every direction. Worse, as he looked down the rockfaces that dizzied away under his feet, he realized that the almost endless verticality put descent out of the question; and, more frightening yet, the lift of his eyes to the skyline revealed that ocean waters were swelling into view, their crests lashing and their advance combers brown with the mud of lands torn up by their onrush, and there could be no doubt that within minutes they were going to start spilling into the great lowland and producing a minor sea which might well engulf the ledge on which he and the two Lexians were standing before the inundation was complete. 'It looks to me,' he said, glancing around at the Lord Chamberlain, 'as if we'll have to turn back.'

'No,' Harbiskoom replied, pointing to the end of the shelf on their right, where a great cornerstone reared its buttress-like support for some overhanging masses of rock about three hundred feet above. 'We can go that way. There is a path.'

Fisher found that hard to believe from the angle at which he was standing; but, as he followed the Lord Chamberlain and Magina Entovitz towards the cornerstone a moment later, he saw that a path was indeed present. It was about a yard wide, rounded the front of the support rock, and had been cut from the spot where the ledge ended and the buttress-shape began. Stepping out and shuffling round it required a little nerve, but nothing more, and the three of them reached the other side of the cornerstone without difficulty.

From here they stepped back on to the greater mountainside again, and now Fisher saw before them a path, partly natural and partly man-made, which dipped and climbed around the eastern face of Purna, vanishing at last in a southward turn which suggested that it might eventually carry them well towards the spaceport on the mountain's opposite side from which the exodus to Earth was taking place.

The watery danger on their left was increasingly apparent, but, after a word or two in recognition of it, Harbiskoom seemed disinclined to pay it much attention and pressed forward again. With the girl moving between him and the Lord Chamberlain, Fisher followed as smartly as he could, but now, as he assessed the length and nature of the path ahead, he felt new misgivings. The vital factor in this was the overall tendency of the track — not so obvious at first — to sink below the level at which they were moving at present. Once more he was conscious of the overwhelming volume of the flood to the east of them, and that it might sweep over all but the mountain's last bastions, and he put the matter to Harbiskoom as strongly as he could, asking if the other didn't know of an alternative route over the mountain or, failing that, through it; but he was told that there was no alternative route over the rock, and that all the tunnels leading to safety, apart from the one that they had used to get up here, had been sealed prior to their leaving Purna's interior. If they were doing the wrong thing, they really had no choice but to go on doing it. Thus they kept forging ahead, and their rapid tread carried them along the edge of precipices, down brief but sudden drops, round more tight corners, across fissures, through long climbs, and on towards the mountain's turn southwards, distance belied by mass and their efforts beginning to seem but slightly rewarded.

The waters from the east were getting close now. It was possible to hear their immense brawling through the booming of the land. Ahead of them drove a cold wind; it whipped and stung at Fisher and the two Lexians and brought a taste of salt with it. Then the great waves curled downwards and rushed into the back of the enormous hollow, meeting the rock of the mountain with a frightful crash and upfling; and after that they thinned and flattened, riding upwards in a dull translucence to form an immensity of shadow which seemed to absorb utterly and to have an unlimited capacity to go on so doing; but, as the minutes went by and the inrush continued, a rising toss of foamcaps set a tangible surface to the forming sea and Purna's lower precipices shortened into splashed travesties of their original hurtling selves and the total mass of the mountain seemed to grow more squat and less majestic.

Forced lower by the physical facts of their route, the three fugitives scrambled for the safety of the higher south, Fisher looking back and down for a time with the regularity of one who felt death hunting him slowly but surely to the kill, but then denying himself so much as a glance at the appalling sight for a much longer period; and it was only when the boiling of the waters impinged upon his eardrums with a near insistence that he took another look and saw for certain that the level at which he and his companions were moving was going to be submerged. He said nothing, for Harbiskoom and the girl had not ceased looking back and were at least as well aware of the situation as he.

Their heads began turning upwards. Dipping nearer to danger with every step, they sought a climb that would carry them to further minutes of safety, but above them the stone was smooth and stepped in such degree that only a giant of inconceivable proportions would have stood a chance of climbing it. They had trapped themselves as surely as Fisher had feared. Their starting point was now the better part of two miles behind them, and to think of retracing their steps was out of the question.

It would have been easier to stop and wait for it, but life's unrelenting urges kept them striving. Then the path rose slightly before them, and they scrambled to a relief that was in the mind alone. From beneath them came the hiss of liquids forcing against stone, and tides raced dizzily along the rockfaces adjacent, carrying trees and vegetation and the debris of civilisation, which included the bodies of animals strange to Fisher and more than one glimpse of a dead and bloated human face.

In front of them now was another descent. But here they had to check; for the rising of the waters had already cut the next stage of their advance. Panting, Fisher set his arms akimbo and raised his eyes to the livid storming that chained the smoky gloom of the uncertain line where the sky and the surface of the planet met. The wind ripped at his scalp, and spray blasted into his face and ran in drenching streams on to his chest and shoulders. Holding his breath, he tried to compose himself. It would not take long. In a minute or two he, Harbiskoom, and Magina Entovitz would be at one with the ten thousand feet of ocean which now swelled almost to their toes.

He put out a hand to the girl. She looked so slight and plastered that he wished to comfort her; but, if she had cried in the Emperor's throne-room, there were no tears about her now; and, as she avoided his touch, he saw on her features a stony resolution to die well. It was rather different with Harbiskoom. He had the tense and frustrated look of an active man who was furious at his inability to help himself further. Yet he, too, was clearly unafraid. The age-old lesson that the brave could die but once seemed to have been well learned on Lexia. But then, of course, it had been a long time in the teaching.

The water washed over Fisher's feet. Its first touch was almost gentle and inviting. Then it spun upwards and hit his knees with the power of a solid, and he twisted off his perch into the forces that swirled at the edge of the flood. He had a momentary glimpse of Harbiskoom and the girl toppling in and struggling near him, but then, with no more than an instant in which to suck a breath, he was forced under and down, and the light faded above his head and he threshed in the drowning silence of the depths believing that he would never rise again; but all at once an upcurrent seemed to catch him and he returned to the surface with no more conscious effort on his part than the arrowing of his hands.

His left shoulder struck something hard, and the big presence of the same unyielding shape forced his head over to the right. Then he saw that he had come up beside the trunk of a floating tree. Seizing a nearby branch, he raised himself high enough in the water to bring the bottom of his ribcage to rest on the limb, and then, blinking and gasping, he peered around him, seeing that he was still in the border race of the rising flood and being borne southwards at a much faster rate than that at which he and the two Lexians had been able to travel on the now submerged mountain path.

The knowledge made him think of the girl and the Lord Chamberlain again. He gazed back and forth across the waters between his tree and Purna's rock, seeking for any sign of Harbiskoom or Magina, but there was no trace of them anywhere; and, after he had lifted himself still higher on the bough and looked across the bole itself to the surface on the east of him — once more without result — he accepted that he was never going to see either of them again; so it came as a happy surprise when a head popped into view on his immediate right and began bobbing up and down on an eddy that brought its half-drowned owner to within touching distance of him.

Fisher reached out with his right hand. His fingers made contact with the cloth of a collar. He grabbed and twisted hard, putting out all his strength as he drew the other in close against the tree. He saw now that the person in his grasp was Harbiskoom, and he heaved the man into a chest-down position over the branch to which he had lately attached himself. The Lord Chamberlain coughed and vomited water, but it was apparent from the returning strength of his grip that he was not too far gone and would soon be able to fend for himself, and presently Fisher removed his guarding hand from the other's back and looked around him again, hoping that fortune might still repeat itself on the girl's behalf, but there was still no sign of her and he shook his head in the sure knowledge that she had by now been under water long enough to have drowned irrevocably; so he put a further outburst of energy into scrambling on to the body of the tree, and after that he leaned over and helped Harbiskoom to a similar position forward of him and astride the trunk. And thereafter, unable to do anything except cling on, they travelled southwards with the tree and rested the shock of their latest experience out of themselves, half an hour passing before the Lord Chamberlain twisted his head around and said: 'Thank you for my life. I will not forget.'

'It was fortunate that you came up so close to me,' Fisher answered. 'I expect it was the same up-current that saved us both. The girl must have been forced straight down.'

Looking to the front again, Harbiskoom nodded sadly. 'She was my niece — my brother's daughter. A girl of strong and faithful character. Tuga Halshafar used her badly. She gave up her family and much else to live as his mistress. Had I not revered the Emperor and loved my brother's child, I would not have gone to the lengths I did to provide for their relationship and keep it secret. Even Trugel Missenheim knew nothing of it, as he likewise knew nothing of the tunnel at the side of the throne-room by which Magina used to visit her love. Besides myself, only Sallus, the deaf mute, knew all the truth, and, leaving out his infirmities, his reverence of the Emperor likewise made the secret safe with him. It was a pity that I had to kill the poor cripple, but he might well have killed Magina and myself had I not fired on him. Earthman, Tuga Halshafar has been better loved and served than he has deserved!'

'My name is Fisher, sir. And what you've just said is so often the case with rulers everywhere. I imagine Halshafar had put Magina from him. He would have done that to make room for me and ensure the success of the substitution.'

'It was about ten days ago.' Harbiskoom replied. 'The poor girl came to me in tears. She told me that the Emperor had informed her that she was not to visit him again. That, in the interests of his remaining duties, he was going to isolate himself from all but his highest ministers and await the end in a state of celibacy. Fortunately for you, if less so for her,

Magina could not bear the idea of her love dying alone, and, as the planet's convulsions moved into their present climactic state, she committed the supreme offence of disobeying a royal command and went to him again through the secret tunnel, intending to plead with him for the last favour of dying in his arms. But she found you, and realized that she had been deceived; and then she came and looked for me, and the rest of the story you know.'

'A moving tale,' Fisher acknowledged. 'But she's out of it now, and, if there's to be no revenge for her, there'll also be no more suffering.'

'I do not believe that she wanted revenge,' Harbiskoom commented. 'She wished to see him exposed as a common mortal.'

'Yes,' Fisher agreed shrewdly. 'On another world, who could object to one common mortal marrying another?'

'It is possible that her mind worked somewhat along those lines,' the Lord Chamberlain conceded, a shiver passing through him and his teeth chattering audibly. 'It will be cold when the darkness comes. Tonight will probably see the end of us.'

Nodding, Fisher looked towards the eastern horizon. There the waters had flattened out of flood, and it seemed that the low lying features of the district had to a large extent contained this latest stage of inundation. The rock-edged tide still bore them southwards, but, with the checking of the flood, it could no longer be an all-powerful current in the ocean's surge, and, once beyond Purna's barrier cliffs and slopes, it was probable that the prevailing westward wash of the waters would carry them towards the spaceport — though this, of course, could already have been washed out or denuded of its last interstellar transport by the time they reached it thanks to the certain speed up of the exodus that the rapidly deteriorating situation must have brought about.

Fisher spoke his thoughts to Harbiskoom again, and the Lord Chamberlain bucked up considerably and admitted that his reasoning could be correct; and then he brought in an additional note of hope by remarking that the vast hollow at their backs was in fact the culmination of a southern land trough which, if shallow for the most part, was hundreds of miles in extent and could have spread the bulk of the inflow over an area that had its stopping point under a long ridge that was situated some distance short of the spaceport. He also added that, with the task of transporting over three hundred thousand emigrants from their hostels outside Kredabah being such a formidable one, he didn't see how the last of the spaceships could possibly get away until after dark; so there was a reasonable chance that the rest of the day lay between them and the need to accept that events had finally condemned them to die on Lexia.

'What time do you think it is?' Fisher asked.

'Mid-afternoon,' Harbiskoom answered. 'I can put it no closer than that. We have perhaps six hours.'

'That should be long enough,' Fisher said, though he didn't feel as confident about it as he sounded.

The drift continued. Fisher could see the southward turn of Purna's rock mass now, and he estimated that they ought to reach it in the next twenty minutes or so; but then the rolling skies above them thickened up still more and a muddy rain began to fall, tiny snakes and other small reptiles descending with it in what Harbiskoom described as 'a lethal shower that must have been sucked up by a whirlwind in the tropics'. The snakes hissed and spat on striking the water around the floating tree, and squid-like things and others that resembled a cross between a lobster and a scorpion showed their fangs and waved their stings, but the two men were lucky enough not to be hit by any of the poisonous creatures and this new cause for fear passed as the last of the reptiles splashed into the water several yards ahead of them and quickly drowned.

But the rain didn't cease. It went on falling steadily. Out of it condensed a sulphurous mist that clung to the surface of the water. Visibility decreased in the reeking murk. Then volcanic ash showered down, its hot presence raising the temperature by many degrees as it sizzled through the atmosphere like a blizzard that replaced snow with cinder dust. The two men crouched under the scorching downfall, crying out and splashing themselves repeatedly as hot fragments burned their flesh and hissed on their sodden clothing.

The air grew thicker yet. It was no longer possible to see much at all. Fisher began to understand the misgiving which had mingled with his recent expression of confidence. An ominous amount of atmospheric activity seemed to be cen-tring on this area. Then a thunderous roar went up far to the left of the floating tree and a column of fire tore out of the depths and momentarily lighted the evil scene for miles around. The world shook; and after that the mountain on the right answered the explosion with an even greater one, and Purna's eastern flank split wide open and multi-coloured tongues of fire jumped out of the fracture and licked the sky, the wound excreting lava as a ponderous shower that splashed down at no great distance beyond the main rockfaces and created fresh movements in the water which lifted the tree bearing the two men and drove it forward at the fastest rate yet.

His eyes fixed on Harbiskoom's back, Fisher clung to the bark between his knees. The fall of the lava went on in their wake, and the forces of propulsion increased steadily. Though, in the arc ahead of him, every trace of land was still hidden by the mephitic atmosphere, Fisher soon realized that, at their present speed of travel, they must already have covered what distance had been left between them and the bend of the mountain and now be crossing the point where the ocean's westward flow should have started pushing them to the right; but there seemed no chance of anything of the sort happening in the presence of the superior impulses raised by the falling lava, and Fisher could only view this further blow to their fortunes in grim taciturnity.

Time went on. The tree kept up its

movement into the south. Fisher's sense of desperation increased with every yard it covered. He and Harbiskoom couldn't go on sitting impotently; something must be done. They must try to change the tree's course for themselves. That ought not to prove impossibly difficult. They were now a long way from the source of the propulsive force which had them in its grip, and he could feel the strength of their motion getting less.

After ascertaining that the Lord Chamberlain could swim — for the facts of the man's rescue from drowning had not proved his ability or the lack of it — Fisher advised the other of what he thought it best for them to do, and they slipped into the water and swam hard to the tree's tip, where they applied such pressure as they could bring to bear and caused the floating shape to turn out of the stream of movement coming from its rear and into the landward drift, which was amply apparent now that the angle of impetus supplied by the tree's weight had been changed.

Satisfied, Fisher helped Harbiskoom

back on to the tree trunk, and was about to climb back himself, when the quantity of debris bumping at his shoulders gave him another idea. He began swimming around in the scum that was closing on the tree, and before long he came upon some broadish slats of wood that appeared almost perfectly suited to what he had in mind. Selecting two of the longest and strongest-looking of the slats, he bore them back to the bole and passed them up to Harbiskoom. 'Paddles,' he explained, as the Lexian took them from his hands.

Now Fisher heaved himself back on to the tree trunk; and after that he and the Lord Chamberlain paddled as hard as they could towards the still invisible land. Around them the gloom thickened as the day lengthened, the rumbling of the earthquakes went on, and volcanic flashes made more of their appearances as weird discolourations in the tight-spun shadows of the north. More and more it became a world of plutonian nightmare, but for Fisher and his companion the challenge was now physical rather than subjective, and they shrugged it off, for it was always easier to meet bodily stresses than to match up to the demands of the fevered mind.

They grounded what must have been more than two hours later. Throwing their paddles aside, they left the tree and waded ashore. Before them a slope covered with moss and dead grasses ran up to a long and occasionally indented ridge which had plainly stood much higher above the terrain at the start of the day, and was obviously the one which Harbiskoom had mentioned. The two men climbed the crest and passed through one of its notches. Still enclosed by fog, they went striding away from the back of the ridge; and, as they put distance between them and the water, the light got better and the banks of mist lifted to the extent that part of Purna became visible on the right and a concrete strip which could only be the eastern boundary of the spaceport appeared directly ahead.

Their steps quickened at the sight of the landing place. Fisher began to wonder if he and Harbiskoom were through the worst, especially as he picked up the sound of a great machine climbing above the far off ground which had been devoted to the interstellar transports; but then a chill wind blasted in from the rear — the almost certain forerunner of a new period of storms — and, as the gusts carried all the intervening fog veils with them, he saw that he and his companion were in fact far from out of their problems; for, over yonder where the mighty fleet of the exodus had lately stood as a ranked body of glittering silver towers, there was now only a scattering of the spaceships left; and, as he bent forward in the blow and watched, two more of these lifted from the ground and vanished through the cloud ceiling, giving him the feeling that the final links with home were soon to disappear and leave him pleading frantically with the empty sky. But all he said was: 'If we run as hard as we're able, we might just get there in time.'

'I overestimated,' the Lord Chamberlain agreed, breaking into a run.

They did well over the first of the five miles which Fisher believed to lie between them and the remaining interstellar transports. The land was very flat and they had the wind at their backs. But after that lack of condition started to tell on them both, and, despite the continued help of the wind, they began to labour and their pace fell off to no more than half of what it had been.

Panting and stumbling, they forced themselves to keep going, Fisher pushing a hand under the older man's right elbow when Harbiskoom threatened to fail. Two more of the last few spaceships lifted off. The sight inspired coldly. A rough count gave it that only seven more of the craft were left. Once again the two men went at it with a desperate energy that threw a killing strain on their unaccustomed hearts and lungs. Fisher sweated in his anxiety. A further two miles fell behind them. They came to a dip where the rains had settled; through the water they splashed. Fisher gulped and blew; Harbiskoom sobbed and croaked; both of them wavered to a stop, then, as three more of the ships took off, got their legs working again.

It was torture. The Lord Chamberlain's face was that of a man who seemed to be dying on his feet. Fisher waved towards the remaining machines, hoping that he and the Lexian would be spotted by a lookout, but there was still more than a mile to go and he was fairly sure that the people aboard the spaceships could have little time for anything but what was happening there. Then his efforts were confounded by another double lift off. That left just two ships standing against the skyline. It was going to turn out as he had feared at first. Harbiskoom and he were going to lose their chance of survival by the smallest of margins.

Heaven displayed a further malice. The rain came down; lightning blazed above them. Then the gods of the earth took the soil in their hands and shook it in further mockery. The ground lurched under Fisher's soles, and a brittle, snapping noise radiated at the greatest speed on all sides of him as the concrete trembled into enormous patterns of hairline cracks and then lifted into irregular ridges of steel-reinforced stone which forced him and his companion to start jumping and dodging in a fashion that could only delay their forward movement by fifteen yards in every hundred. It seemed as if the entire landing space were about to break up, and that every power inimical to their continued existence was now bent against them; for, hearing a roar that was other than the wind in his wake, Fisher threw back the fastest of glances and saw the sea foaming over the ridge that he and the Lord Chamberlain had crossed about half an hour ago. Even if a lookout should spot them now, what captain in his right senses, with such a sight to discourage him, would delay his ship's departure in order to take them aboard. They might just as well stroll it until the sea caught up with them: for they were indeed beaten. And, as the nearer of the two remaining transports left the planet's surface, Fisher felt the more certain of it.

But even now it was not in them to give up. The very difficulties seemed to bring out their final reserves of strength and willpower. With heads thrown back and their arms pumping, they pelted, sprang and dodged, and the last spaceship loomed through the rain like the symbol of a new dawn. Then, as he pushed a final bunch of people on to the platform of his elevator, the man in charge of passenger loading spotted them and beckoned with huge and urgent sweeps of his right arm. After that the sound of his voice forced against the wind and the mounting thunder of the oncoming flood, and his thin ill-temper piped the ultimate in compelling inspiration. Then his hands seized the runners by the slack cloth on their chests and pulled; and next they were on the elevator — and then they were in the doorway of the spaceship; and, lastly, in the instant before the hatch slammed shut and the machine took off, Fisher saw the great waters within a few hundred yards of the craft and heard their frustrated roar at being cheated.

It had been close. He prayed to God that nothing would ever be quite so close again.

9

As one of the three hundred people packed into the smallest of the space-ship's holds, Fisher spent much of the period journeying towards Earth in recovering from the exhaustion that the final hours of his brief stay on Lexia had induced in him, and in thinking about whatever lay directly ahead. He would have liked to talk the matter over with the Lord Chamberlain, but Harbiskoom — who sat on the floor at his side, shoulderblades to the bulkhead and feet outstretched — was too fast asleep for that. What they needed was a plan of action, for it was obvious that, no matter what happened when they disembarked in New Lexia and lost the anonymity of the present crush and their dishevelment, they were going to find themselves with some complex problems. The first of these — assuming that he was to co-operate in the manner that he believed the Lord Chamberlain wished of him — would be to keep clear of those who would be likely to recognise him as Craig Fisher and had the need to maintain Tuga Halshafar in that identity. This would be necessary to insure that Harbiskoom could pick his own time and circumstances in which to reveal the plot to leave a substitute Emperor on Lexia and thus make the maximum capital out of it. After that must come the closely allied need to change his appearance as much as he possibly could and avoid all public activities that might bring him to the least prominence and cause the more observant of the rank-and-file Lexians to remark on his resemblance to Halshafar. For the rest, he would have to rely on Harbiskoom to feed, house, and direct him, since the other would still have total freedom of movement and the unquestioned power of his position to cover everything he did. Yes, it was all very tenuous and ominously plastic, and would plainly react with too great a readiness to the first real shaping force or influence with which it came in contact.

But, if he feared the unpredictability of the immediate future, he knew that others too were going to be moved to largely instinctive reactions by the confusion in the too suddenly over-populated New Lexia, and he saw in that the sure breeding ground of opportunism. He wished that his subconscious would not keep reminding him that neither the Lexians nor their ruler were as high-minded as they would like to believe themselves to be; for he could see one rather obvious base action whereby Tuga Halshafar could solve at a single throw all the personal and political problems arising from the substitution, especially the enmity to his presence — either as the Emperor or Craig Fisher — from the New Lexian war faction, and also appear to be doing a difficult best for those of his people who might be seriously disappointed or outraged by the duplicity to which he had lent himself. But Fisher decided not to dwell on that, for he had often noticed that evil ideas were the most mentally transmissible. Having taken what precautions he could, he would have to leave events to work themselves out. Too much thought along too many lines could lead to a dangerous lack of spontaneity in reactions.

With the slowing down of his brain, Fisher's nerves and muscles relaxed, and he slept too; and he did not awake until the nasal rasping of a crewman's voice burst on his eardrums from a loudspeaker above his head. Yawning, he shifted against the bulkhead at his back and saw that Harbiskoom was also awake and staring at him. He perceived a questioning, calculating light in the Lord Chamberlain's eye, and judged that the other — probably without knowing as much as he about the set up in New Lexia — had been having some of the thoughts which had exercised him earlier, and, giving a quick nod, he smiled and asked: 'What was that fellow on the ship's intercom saying?'

'We are out of warp,' Harbiskoom answered, 'and are due to reach journey's end in about five minutes. The man was asking for an orderly disembarkation. Messages from New Lexia suggest that they have enough disorder down there already.'

'Inevitably,' Fisher commented, noting that one or two of the people around them were taking a vague interest in the use of the English tongue. 'We'd better shut up. It would be unwise to call too much attention to me.'

'Agreed,' Harbiskoom said; and they became silent.

The ship touched down shortly after that. People stirred, and those who were sitting or lying got to their feet. There was a tense and expectant mutter of voices where there had been dead silence a few minutes ago. Rising himself, as Harbiskoom got up stiffly beside him, Fisher gazed at the rings of light in the ceiling, the unadorned commonplace of the sheet metal walls, and the perforated ventilation points in the cornices. He dismissed a tremor of unreality. It seemed impossible that, in such a simple chamber, the miracle of crossing fifteen light years had again been achieved. It was almost like wishing yourself between worlds. But then the Lexians did step outside material reality to do it.

It was night outside. This, perhaps, made the disembarkation slower than it might have been; though, as Fisher gazed out through the main hatch, from the rear of the queue in the corridor at the approaches to it, he had a feeling that the chief trouble was in the reluctance of this last body of the Lexian exodus to suffer the birth pangs of emerging from the womblike certainty of the spaceship into the thousand problems of making a new life on another world; but score by score the elevator carried the unhappy-looking people to the ground, and it finally came the turn of Fisher and Harbiskoom to step out on to the platform and be carried downwards through the white brilliance of the many arc lights that were in play among the close-packed, towering shapes of the interstellar craft that ringed their own vessel round and extended like a forest of steel boles into the back of the night.

Stepping from the elevator's floor on to terra firma, Fisher gave his right foot a solid stamp to express his satisfaction in being home, and then he tried to settle a course of progress for the Lord Chamberlain and himself amidst the milling, aimless surges of people who were passing among the rounded bases of the nearer and, in all probability, most recently arrived of the spaceships. A continuous broadcast was coming from a battery of loudspeakers situated somewhere on the left — almost certainly from outside the spaceport's terminal building — but the patient insistence of the voice that kept repeating itself seemed to be achieving little of any sort in resolving the chaos of souls; and Fisher was about to take hold of Harbiskoom's sleeve and begin shouldering a path for them towards the booming voice, when out of the white robed press came a man wearing a natty raincoat, shoes with pointed toes, and a Tyrolean hat. He was waving an umbrella in the air and calling the Lord Chamberlain's name. 'Why, Mr. Hento,' Fisher murmured.

Though Hento had undoubtedly seen and recognised Fisher, he was simply not interested in him for the moment. His eyes were all for Harbiskoom, and he gave vent to an expression of delight as he first bowed to the Lord Chamberlain and then embraced him. Harbiskoom returned the embrace, slapping Hento on the back, and then they broke apart and stood at arm's-length, jabbering happily to one another; and, knowing that Hento's appearance very likely meant that it would be better for him to make a quick disappearance while he had the chance, Fisher began to slide away into the crowd; but Hento caught sight of his movement and promptly seized him by the arm, hanging on with just sufficient firmness to make it plain that it would be to his advantage to stay where he was. 'So, Mr. Fisher,' he said. 'I did not expect to see you back.'

'Your words mean that you know the truth of what has happened,' Fisher said narrowly.

'About the substitution, yes,' Hento confirmed.

Then, despite his previous display of friendliness towards the man, Harbiskoom took on a wary look and said: 'This is a disgraceful business, Hento. I cannot believe that my favourite pupil from the great college for inter-planetary agents can have lent himself to it willingly.'

'I did not know that the substitution was being planned,' Hento protested. 'I am merely a servant, my Lord Chamberlain. I do as I am told — as I always did when you were my principal in Kredabah.'

'Have you learned of the substitution as a matter of observation?' Fisher asked. 'Or has the Emperor revealed himself?'

'He has revealed himself,' Hento replied, casting a rather furtive glance about him. 'I ought to arrest you, Mr. Fisher; but, as you and my old teacher are obviously together, I have a feeling that he would prefer it otherwise. Thus, for our safety, the three of us cannot talk here. I have a car parked near the terminal building. We will go to my room in Project House. This way.'

Hento threaded a rapid path through the drifting crowds. He led Harbiskoom and Fisher to the eastern edge of the clustered spaceships. After that he kept to the thickest of the shadows beyond the concentrated glare of the arc lights and made for the parking space that was visible on the right of the terminal building. Here they came at once to the vehicle of which he had spoken, and he opened its top and motioned for Fisher and the Lord Chamberlain to sit down on the back seat, which they did; and then he got in himself, locked down the transparent cover, started the electric motor, and left the park by the northern exit lane, turning right at its end and joining the road on which Fisher had travelled to the spaceport with Arle and Varinia before leaving for Lexia. There was a certain amount of traffic about, but the crowds of emigrants had not strayed this far from the spaceships, so, taking account of the conditions, it was still possible to travel pretty fast, and it wasn't long before the brightly lighted presence of Project House and the buildings in its vicinity became apparent on the not too distant flatness of the night-clad land. 'I was worried about you, Most Honourable Harbiskoom,' Hento said, breaking the five minutes old silence in a rather abrupt manner.

'I thank you, Hento,' the Lord Chamberlain replied.

'I have been watching the spaceships in,' Hento went on. 'I believe yours was the last of them.'

'It was,' Harbiskoom said. 'Mr. Fisher and I joined it only moments before lift-off.'

'I have been told that it was difficult towards the end.'

'It was difficult for everybody,' Harbiskoom agreed. 'We must remember those who were given no choice but to die.'

'The lot of the second class citizens,' Hento observed, regretfully but also with a dismissive note.

'Betrayed by Tuga Halshafar nevertheless.'

'As you say, Most Honourable Harbiskoom,' Hento concurred, clearly still of no mind to be drawn beyond the admission.

'How do you come to be in New Lexia, Mr. Hento?' Fisher asked, watching the car's headlights slice across a corner. 'I had the perhaps false idea that you agents were employed almost without rest in the affairs of the outside world.'

'We are on recall just now,' Hento answered evasively.

'New strategies in the formation?'

'Wait,' Hento counselled; then, in a sudden flash of perhaps promptly regretted revelation, he continued: 'I have to be sure in my own mind what I am doing. The Most Honourable Harbiskoom may well have need of the best advice that I can give him. I alone have all the facts he needs.'

Fisher's jaws snapped shut. The words had a cautionary ring to them. It had been one thing for Harbiskoom to speak of Tuga Halshafar in revengeful tones during the heat of a Lexian moment; but he might well feel differently about the matter if he were made to realize that the situation in New Lexia was such that any word or action against the Emperor would find no favour anywhere and bring about his death. Though a man of feeling and principles, he might be persuaded that the sacrifice of an Earthman to the Emperor was no more than recognition of the inevitable. Fisher perceived that he could feel secure in no Lexian's friendship, and that Hento would automatically be disposed to play a sharp game on behalf of a friend and superior.

They reached Project House. Fisher put his worries aside as the car pulled up in a road on the southern side of the building which counterbalanced that with which he had previously become familiar on the north. He saw that a large vehicle had stopped about forty yards ahead of them, and that several unkempt persons who could only be immigrants had lately got out of it and were now entering the building on the left. The population of New Lexia having increased by well over three hundred thousand in the last day, it went without saying that a taxi service had distributed many of them about the district during that period, and that Project House — not over-filled in his experience — must have taken its share of them. 'Can you be sure that you still have a room to yourself?' Fisher asked Hento, as he and Harbiskoom stepped out of the car at the agent's back. 'It looks to me as if you could find yourself with lodgers.'

'There is no fear of that,' Hento answered, leading them through a small door which was situated on the car's immediate left — many yards short of the buttress-type entrance through which the immigrants had just vanished — and on to a steep flight of granite steps that led into the basement of Project House. 'An agent is helped and encouraged to maintain his privacy at all times — not least during those of crisis.'

They came to the foot of the steps. Here Hento turned right and followed the main corridor which they had entered for the distance of a pace or two, after which he turned into a passage on the left and moved into a dormitory area, where he took out a key and unlocked the first door on the right, switching on the light as he motioned for his companions to enter the room beyond ahead of him. Harbiskoom went in first, and Fisher crossed the threshold on the Lord Chamberlain's heels, Hento quickly bringing up the rear and shutting the door securely at their backs.

Fisher looked around him. They were in a small bed-cum-sitting room of the kind that he had himself occupied on the other side of the basement, though this one possessed the additional comforts of being carpeted throughout and having a couch and a sideboard.

'Sit down,' Hento invited, indicating the couch. 'Wine?'

Both Harbiskoom and Fisher nodded, seating themselves, and their host went to the sideboard and filled two goblets from the decanter standing there. Then he carried the drinks to his guests and put the goblets into their outstretched hands. 'You must have guessed what happened,' he said. 'Once on this world, the disguised Emperor hid his real identity for only as long as it took Trugel Missenheim to make sure that the stronger ground in New Lexia was occupied by those who wish to subjugate rather than ask sanctuary of the indigenous peoples of the Earth; and after that Halshafar came straight into the open and announced that he had come to this planet to give the people of the exodus the benefit of his great leadership in the conquest of the Earth and the establishment of the kind of caste system which had made them supreme at home. Doctor Samerle and Khaka stepped forward as the leaders of the war faction here. They at once declared their acceptance of the Emperor's leadership, and the government leaders who had already arrived from Lexia followed up by doing the same. Then the great majority of the rank-and-file expressed their willingness to accept the arrangement, and there was really nothing more to be said.'

'Only Arle and a handful of his close friends decried what was happening. It stayed their contention that, even allowing for our superior weapons and knowledge, the sheer weight of numbers that we must come up against would defeat us in the end and make our anihilation a virtual certainty. He, his daughter and his friends, are now under arrest in this building. Thus, Most Honourable Harbiskoom, if you had thoughts of showing up Tuga Halshafar for the cowardly trickster that he undoubtedly is, you may forget them. Our Emperor has covered his blemishes, and New Lexia is committed to war under his command. And there is nothing that you or any man can do to prevent it.'

'You spoke of your advice, Hento,' the Lord Chamberlain said. 'What is it?'

'Hand Mr. Fisher over to the Emperor. Say nothing, and do whatever is asked of you.'

'What would happen to Mr. Fisher?'

'If you were Tuga Halshafar, what would you do to the living reminder of your duplicity?'

'It shall not be,' Harbiskoom said in a quiet but strong voice. 'Mr. Fisher saved my life on Lexia. I will not see his taken.'

Hento gave a nod that both understood and approved. 'He must hide as best he may. Let him stay away from us, and we will forget him. Harsh, perhaps, but the best for us all. He will at least have a chance of life.'

'Thank you,' Fisher said. 'I'm not insensible of the risk you're taking in the name of friendship, Mr. Hento. May I ask you a question?'

'Go ahead,' Hento replied, a cynical shift in his eye telling that he didn't guarantee an answer.

'Do you approve of your people going to war against the nations of the Earth?'

'No,' Hento answered. 'I agree with Arle. The numbers against us are too great. Any thinking man should be able to see that. Also, as I who have been among them have the best reason to know, your races are neither as technologically backward nor lacking in craft and courage as men like Doctor Samerle and Khaka have persuaded themselves to believe. I am convinced that we have far more to gain from asking than fighting. Here again, I am better qualified than most to judge.'

'That's definite enough,' Fisher remarked. 'Would you be prepared to help me prevent this war?'

'That makes it a different matter,' Hento said. 'I could not possibly help you without betraying my own kind. But what remains more to the point is that I do not see anything that you could do — or say — to prevent what is coming. You are one man, and here, at least, the Lexians are many.'

'I'd stake that the great majority of them are worried sick,' Fisher returned; 'and, because of it, malleable in the highest degree. If we could remove the evil leaders and replace them with better men, we could reverse the present situation.'

'Remove?' Hento said sharply. 'You imply force. No matter how badly I might disagree with those set above me, I would never lift a hand against them.'

'Force is the only way,' Fisher assured him. 'I think I may be able to acquire the hands, if you can help out with a little information.'

'First tell me where the hands are to come from,' Hento urged, a jeering note in his voice that suggested that the Earthman might be thinking of spiriting them in.

'There's a black mound north of here,' Fisher answered. 'I have good reason to believe that you keep the men and machines there stolen by you from the outside world.'

'Now that could be,' Hento acknow-ledged, a new respect dawning in his eye as a deeply thoughtful expression came over his features generally. 'Could you guarantee that no Lexian would get hurt? Of course you could not. Those captive Earth-people have no love of their jailors.'

'We have a saying, Mr. Hento,' Fisher persisted soberly. 'You can't make an omelette without first breaking the eggs.'

'I have heard your foolish saying,' Hento said irritably.

'Then try another,' Fisher said, slightly incensed. 'You achieve nothing by sitting on the fence.'

'This is madness!' Hento declared.

'It would be a greater madness to make war,' Harbiskoom said with an authority that brooked no argument. 'Why do you trouble your conscience? The men who would risk the wiping out of our people have in that folly lost the right to any loyalty from you and me.'

'The Most Honourable Harbiskoom makes it very plain where he stands,'

Hento observed bitterly. 'Very well. If you can get the men, Mr. Fisher, there is a situation in which the guilty leaders can be taken together this very night.' He looked at the watch on his left wrist. 'At two a.m. — that is about three hours from now — Tuga Halshafar, Missenheim, Doctor Samerle, and Khaka will be sitting together in a room not far from here. They will be at the controls of the fire-blaster. It is their intention to burn out the Pentagon, the Kremlin, the Ministry of Defence in London, and the Imperial City of Peking as their first offensive action against the Earth-people.'

'They're not giving the Lexians time to think,' Fisher mused. 'All right. First I have to get into the mound.'

'I may be able to help you in that also,' Hento said in the strained voice of a man who was still fighting a great inner battle with himself. 'I know the place very well, from visits there to interrogate the Earth prisoners in years gone by. To enter by the front door is out of the question. The mound, as you call it, is well if not heavily guarded. Your only hope of getting into it alive is through the main ventilation shaft. This is situated fairly low and well towards the front on the western side of it. Fortunately, it comes out in the guards' living quarters and — '

'Fortunately?' Fisher interrupted.

'For our purpose, yes,' Hento said, allowing himself the thinnest of smiles. 'One of the advantages of being an agent is that one has access to certain articles that are not available to everybody. Gas bombs of a special kind for instance.' He went to his bed and pulled out a case from under it, giving instructions as he raised its lid and removed a number of items which he kept hidden near his right knee. 'Time,' he concluded, 'is obviously your worst enemy. To take a car — even with the idea of parking it at a distance from your objective — would be to invite discovery, so you will have to travel to the mound and back on foot. That means a cross country round trip of perhaps eight miles. You must try to avoid hold ups. If you fail to stop the Emperor and his confederates from destroying the military centres of the four greatest powers on

Earth, I fear war may prove unavoidable whatever happens later.'

Fisher had to agree. The leaders of the Earth would be unlikely to treat with aliens who could put their dreadful weapons to such sudden and treacherous use. The recent past was too full of tyrants and surprise attacks for that.

10

Moving at the trot, Fisher crossed the open ground between two patches of New Lexian woodland, the mound for which he was heading the darkest of blurs on a black skyline that was dusted with stars and touched by the low-slanting rays of the lately risen moon.

During the last few days a sense of his own inadequacy had often come to him, but just now he hardly dared think of the size and responsibility of the job that he had undertaken. Apart from some quick descriptions that Hento had provided — and a conducted glimpse of the door through which he would need to pass in the basement of Project House in order to complete the night's work — he had set himself to bring down the most powerful of the aliens and some of their best servants in places that were quite unknown to him. To this end he had in his possession two thickish glass balls which contained, so Hento had assured him, a quick-clearing sporific gas of long lasting effect, a mask to protect him against the gas, a one hundred foot length of nylon rope with a small grapnel fixed to one end and a lead weight to the other, and a wristwatch to provide him with time synchronised to that which the Emperor and his confederates would be using. The equipment was about as inadequate as Hento's help had been carefully limited to prevent Fisher's doing any lasting harm to the guards in the mound, and the danger that failure might occur for no other reason than that the level of effort was forced to match the interplanetary agent's reluctance to help at all could not be discounted. If only the man had provided a weapon with which to threaten, the chances would have been greatly improved — as would have been even more true had he been prepared to come along and provide the practical benefits of his experience where they were most needed — but he had carefuly stopped short at the point where all the work and risks fell the Earthman's lot. Yet if that were hypocritical, perhaps it was also natural, for equipment could always have been stolen from him, and, so long as he wasn't actually present if anything went wrong, it would be hard to prove that he had played an active part in Fisher's doings. After all, his help had been given under Harbiskoom's influence, and it was a fair certainty that he would have had nothing to do with the business and seen the Earthman locked up if it had not been for the Lord Chamberlain's presence. One had to make full allowances, particularly as the agent had obviously been assisting a purpose that he did not believe could be achieved.

The air was balmy, and the night still. Progress went on coming easily. Fisher found the present exercise an aid to muscles stiffened on Lexia and a good unwinder of overstrung nerves. The mound drew nearer, and, keeping well to the left of the runway that served the huge doors in the face of the formation, he crossed the concrete road which curved across the front of the area and approached the mound closely, looking now for possible sentries; but he saw nobody and the sinister bulge of the land soon dwarfed him entirely and the increasing warmness of the air reminded him of how near he was to the atmospheric cycle on which New Lexia depended for its clement weather conditions.

He began climbing the side of the mound on his right. The slant of the formation forced him to more effort than he had expected. He started to sweat, and the heaviness of the Lexian garments that he was still wearing was no help in the matter. After a certain amount of quartering, he located the ventilation shaft of which Hento had spoken and looked down through the grille which covered its head. He spotted a glimmer of light far below him, and, listening intently, picked up a faint sound of laughter. There was unquestionably a room down there, and men in it; and, seeing no reason for further delay, he carefully lifted the metal grille out of its stone frame and pushed it far enough back from the nearer side of the shaft's top to admit his body. Then he removed the nylon rope from a big pocket in the side of his robe, attached the grapnel to the edge of the grille opposite him, and placed the lead-loaded end of the rope on the brink of the shaft near his right foot. Next he pulled on his gasmask, and then he took out one of his gas bombs and hurled it into the depths, hearing a small, glassy pop as it burst at the bottom of the drop a second or so later. Then, pushing the lead weight into space, he felt its chuck at the grapnel as the rope unwound to its full length without reaching the foot of the shaft.

The fact of the deficiency was disquieting, for it created the uncertainty of a final drop, but Fisher could not allow himself to think about that. Getting a firm grip on the very thin rope, he swung into the shaft and then began to lower himself into the depths, the night sky receding to a dimmer and dimmer blur above his head as his confidence increased and his hand-over-hand descent grew faster with it; then, with a suddenness that took him by surprise, he found himself at the rope's end and his feet dangling into the space that he had feared, and there was nothing for it but to let go — which he did, shutting his eyes and relaxing as much as he could; and almost instantly his soles found a standing place amidst the crunch of broken glass from the gas bomb, and he exhaled a sigh of relief in the knowledge that his final drop had been one of not more than three feet. So far, so good; things were really going about as well as could be expected.

Standing at the shaft's centre, Fisher breathed slowly and deeply, making sure that his mask was still forming a proper fit and that he could breathe through it without difficulty. Then, satisfied that all was as it should be, he crouched down, already aware of a slotted continuation of the shaft through the wall on his left and the emergence from it of the glimmer of light which he had first seen through the trap above. The slot was about two and a half feet high and perhaps four wide — just big enough to admit a kneeling man — and Fisher faced round, lowered himself on to all fours, and eased himself into it sideways, coming to a position in which a wall blocked his further movement to the right and his eyes looked out through a perforated duct cover into a kind of barrack room, where quantities of reddish fumes were wreathing slowly above a stone floor on which lay the unconscious shapes of several men dressed in black and white uniforms.

Fisher gave the cover a good push with his hands. It moved in its frame and then resisted; but a second and stronger push popped it out of its bed and it fell to the floor of the room beyond. After that, shuffling his feet forward, he brought himself to a sitting position with his legs dangling down the wall, and finally he projected his lower body forward and stood out into the barrack room.

Breathing heavily in his mask, Fisher began stepping over the inert figures on the floor and avoiding the lockers and beds that lined the gangways present. He went to the door on the other side of the room, and, after dragging a couple of senseless men away from it, opened up and looked out. Beyond him stretched an inadequately lighted passage. This appeared to be deserted, and he stepped into it and tiptoed rapidly to its further end, where it joined a broad rock ledge which had a protective rail that ran along its outer edge. Shouldering up to the corner of the passage on his left, Fisher peeped out, first to the right and then in the opposite direction, still seeing nobody, and after that he stepped out to the centre of the ledge and craned towards the protective rail, seeing beyond it a cavern of a gloomy and yawning vastness which seemed to take up almost the entire interior of the mound. Then, drawn by a curiosity that was as great as his fear of being seen, he went up to the rail and looked over it, the floor below offering a sight that he had thought would be there. Dimly illuminated by the roof's sleeved lighting were the shapes of numerous aircraft, large and small — military and otherwise — cars, lorries, a number of small sea-going vessels, and many examples of non-mobile machinery that could have had to do with space and nuclear programmes: the whole forming an extensive and untended proof of the thefts which the Lexians had perpetrated from the Earth's skies, roadways, and most secret installations for well over a generation.

Hento had told Fisher that the Earth-people captured at the time of these thefts were imprisoned in cells excavated behind the galleries at the back of the mound. Fisher began following the ledge to the left. Certain that the gas cloud which he had caused to enter the barrack room could not have extended its influence this far, he removed the gasmask from his face and pushed it into his pocket. Able to see with more clarity now that the circles of transparency had gone from before his eyes, Fisher realized that the inside of the mound was a little less gloomy than it had previously seemed, and, allowing no break in his movement, he cast another glance across the scene below and then screwed his head round until he had in view the great doors that formed much of the mound's front and the lighted window of a room cut into the rock on their right which was no doubt that occupied by the guards who watched the entrance. Then he drew his gaze back through the arc which it had just travelled, taking in every detail, for it was essential to familiarise himself with the cavern's lay-out while he had the chance. Provided he met with success in what he had come to do, it would be necessary for him and the captives that he had released to leave the mound by the front door. Hento had told him that it was the only way in and out of the mound in normal use, and it would certainly be too much to ask men weakened by imprisonment to climb a hundred feet up a nylon rope. But he must not look too far ahead; the chance of failure was much greater than that of success.

He saw that he was nearing the end of the ledge. An opening in the rear wall of the cavern appeared to provide the next stage of his path to the zone in which the prisoners were held. But then a movement in a concealed watch place near the corner formed by the cavern's back and the wall which ran along the rear of the ledge took him by surprise, and he almost stopped in his tracks as a uniformed man who was armed with a shock-pistol stepped out into his path and viewed him with puzzlement. His heart speeding, Fisher walked on as jauntily as he could, for he was not unaware of the disguising aspects of his Lexian garments and white hair, and he smiled and moved his lips to further the deception. He was within ten feet of the guard before the man gave way to a suspicious peering, and, knowing that the colour of his eyes had finally betrayed him, Fisher jumped across the remaining gap with his left fist flashing out. The blow thumped on the side of the Lexian's jaw, and he lurched backwards and began to fall, two more punches to the chin helping his descent, but he was a strong man and obviously no worse than stunned as he lay propped on his elbows; so the Earthman had no choice but to snatch the shock-pistol from his hands and finish reducing him to unconsciousness with a blow from the weapon's barrel.

Then Fisher went on through the opening in the cavern's rear wall. He held the shock-pistol before him as he bent into the slight descent of the shadowy tunnel before him. He felt a good deal more confident now, and knew that the odds against him were a trifle less formidable. Now he could threaten, and, if necessary, defend himself; but he recognised the vital need to avoid killing if he could. It was in the spilling of blood that you created the future's enmities.

Presently the passage Fisher was walking joined a cross corridor of much larger dimensions. Here a disagreeable smell which he recognised as that of long-enclosed humanity reached him, and, wrinkling his nostrils, he looked from left to right and back again, taking in four arches in the corridor's opposite wall that gave access to what appeared to be the same number of big square rooms which had metal-studded doors with grilles set in their upper parts situated at intervals around the walls. Here, quite clearly, was the Lexian prison area, and, as Fisher began working from one chamber to the next — moving from left to right and seeking guard or guards — he suddenly realized, from the packed human sounds coming from the cells, that there were far too many captives about the prison to consider freeing them all at this time, for he saw now that he needed no more than two dozen to carry through his stealthy plan to frustrate the Lexian warmakers in the basement of Project House, and that a mass release would lead to the kind of undisciplined noise and chaos which he could most do without.

He located the guards in the last of the rooms. There were four of them. They were leaning against the far wall and yarning together after the fashion of men doing a job which they had come to regard as a necessary bore. Sidestepping across the threshold, he called their attention to him in English, and they stared first at him in disbelief and then his weapon; but it was not until he had walked right up to them and his eyes had again betrayed his racial identity that they accepted the threat as real and one of them tried to jump to a knob that protruded from a baseplate which was attached to the wall that separated prison room and corridor, his intention plainly to set off an alarm which would be heard all over the mound and bring its guards running; but Fisher made an interception with his left leg, and, as the other tripped over it, again used the barrel of his shock-pistol as a club, instantly reducing the over-zealous ergo-man to an inert heap on the floor.

Then, daring the other three aliens to move a finger, Fisher shouted: 'Are there any young English-speaking men among you prisoners in here?'

There was a long pause. Then, from the middle cell of the three situated on the right, a voice with an American-sounding accent said: 'The name's Huggins. I've got a number of fellows with me who answer to your description. Who the hell are you anyway, mister?'

'My name's Fisher,' Fisher replied, making out the pale blur of the speaker's crown behind the bars in the door of the cell from which the voice had come. 'I'm an Englishman, and I want to be in this place as little as I imagine you do. My purpose is to form a commando capable of doing a vital job and of getting us all out of New Lexia. Are you game, Huggins?'

'Just give me the chance!' came the harsh reply.

'And me,' another voice grated.

'Same here!' called a third.

Numerous other voices from Huggins' cell then added to the chorus.

'Thank you,' Fisher said; and then he made it clear to the three Lexians in front of his shock-pistol that he wanted Huggins' door opened, and one of the trio bent his head over the unconscious man on the floor and removed the key-ring from his belt. Then, carrying the ring to the door in question, he found the key that fitted the lock and rattled a turn, Huggins pushing out into the main chamber with the decisiveness of a man who was very sure of himself and his own mind. 'Nice to meet you,' Fisher assured him, approving the other's square build, craggy brow, clear blue eyes and golden beard.

'God dammit!' Huggins exploded, looking Fisher up and down with a dawning hatred. 'We've been had for suckers! You're one of those Lexian bastards!'

'Don't jump to conclusions!' Fisher advised, noting that eleven young men had now appeared at Huggins' back and that he and they all wore Air Force blue. 'Come over to the light and take a good look at my eyes.'

'He's a Limey all right, Hug,' declared a lanky fellow who was as dark as the other was fair.

'Who asked you to put your oar in, Coulter?' Huggins snapped, his tones quite definitely those of the man who gave the orders. 'He looks enough like one of them to be one; but, taking it all round, I guess we'd better give him the benefit of the doubt.'

'It would be wise,' Fisher agreed. 'Are you men from the Royal Canadian Air Force?'

'Two two eight Squadron,' Huggins acknowledged, a sliver of doubt remaining in his manner. 'Harriers. I was the squadron leader. What's your story?'

'It's much too long to tell.' Fisher looked at his wristwatch. 'We have under two hours in which to save much of our world from being depopulated and burned to ashes.'

'I've been taking bent pennies all my life,' Huggins said flatly. 'We want to know more than we know right now. You had better tell us some of it, Fisher.'

Fisher saw that he must. He gave an account of the events that had led to his coming to New Lexia, told of his subsequent journeying across space, and briefly outlined what must now be done in the basement of Project House. It all sounded sketchy, disjointed, and incredible; but, despite his initial attitude, Huggins didn't demur at any of it, and he finally said: 'Okay. It's all crazy enough to fit with how my squadron was sucked out of the sky back in Seventy eight and the rest of our folk got here. God, but you've had your luck! Just to walk in here — '

'To borrow from your own parlance,' Fisher interrupted — 'you don't know the half of it. Tell your men to push those guards into the cell you just came out of. There's an unconscious man lying at the head of the passage that leads through from the cavern to this prison place. Send a couple of men to carry him through here. And have the unconscious man over by the wall dragged into the cell too. Take any arms you can find on them before you lock them in.'

Huggins gave three or four orders that more-or-less echoed Fisher's words, and, as his men scattered and began to carry them out, he turned to Fisher again and asked: 'What else do you want?'

For a moment Fisher was uncertain; his mind had gone on amending. 'I had been reckoning on another ten or twelve young men. English-speaking, of course, and able to think for themselves.'

'That ought to be easy,' Huggins growled, 'but I'm damned if I see it being so. They're scattered thin. It will mean unlocking every cell in this rat-hole. You've got people of all ages and races in here, and I figure that'd bring you a general crash-out I don't see you wanting right now.'

'I've done some tentative thinking on this,' Fisher said. 'I haven't mentioned it until now, but, before we can leave the mound, we have to contend with the guardroom at the big doors. For what I know, there may be other guards about too. A rabble is the last thing we need; silence is a must.' He made his decision. 'All the people who are still locked up will have to stay locked up for the present. We'll have to make the most of the men we've got.'

'They are the best,' Huggins assured him. 'Two two eight was a crack squadron.'

'Which could very well be the reason why its disappearance was kept from the world,' Fisher commented, hardening himself to ignore the increasing number of voices, mostly speaking broken English, that were demanding to be let out of the cells.

Shortly after that the two men who had been sent to fetch the unconscious Lexian from the head of the link passage came in with their burden. The alien was dumped in the open cell with the other four, and then Huggins gave himself the obvious pleasure of locking them in. Then, with no further word among themselves — but followed by more and louder cries to be let out from the prisoners nearby — Fisher, Huggins, and the other eleven men left the room and soon joined the passage that gave access to the great cavern which formed the heart of the mound.

A minute later they came to the ledge that traversed the upper western wall of the hollow place. A deep silence still hung in the spaces above the ageing machines on the floor below. Pausing momentarily, Fisher leaned over the protective rail on the left and looked towards the guard-room, where the light still burned steadily in the window set into the rock on the right of the enormous doors. He could detect no movement, either in or out of the place, and whispered an encouraging word to his companions as he led on again. The more torpid the guards, the easier they would be to deal with.

A padding run brought the party to the further end of the ledge. Now a descending passage was visible in the wall beyond. A stairway threaded through the tunnel's tight left-hand curve. This they descended and emerged in an alcove at ground level, Fisher seeing the guardroom in the wall on their right and not thirty feet ahead of them. Crouching, he beckoned to the others and began a darting movement that carried him under the room's window level and across the front of its closed door, the impetus of his steps ceasing only as he reached the nearer leaf of the great doors and straightened in the presence of their soaring girders and the well-oiled machinery which had clearly been installed to provide for their opening from the room in the wall nearby. The Canadian airmen, breathing a trifle heavily, bunched up at his back, and he was about to tell them to remain where they were while he back-tracked and did what had to be done in the matter of the guardroom, when he saw a smaller door at the side of the large one and realized that it must be used to enable the ergo-men to pass in and out of the mound without the greater doors having to be opened. 'Take your men outside, Squadron Leader,' he whispered, pointing to the side door. 'I'll join you shortly.'

Huggins looked at him inquiringly, then pushed the door open. In the same moment the clangour of an alarm bell came from the guardroom, and Fisher muttered under his breath as he guessed that the movement of the door had brought the response. 'Keep going!' he urged; and then he took the second gas bomb from his pocket and ran towards the guardrom, where he could now hear plenty of movement going on.

The door of the guardroom opened as Fisher reached it, and an ergo-man stopped face to face with him on the threshold. The alien was armed, and could have blasted the Earthman where he stood, but his was another case of being deceived by Fisher's white hair and Lexian garments, and he hesitated long enough in the use of his shock-pistol for the Earthman to give him a shove backwards that caused him to crash into a table at which a second man was sitting at an apparatus which looked like some form of radio-telephone. Crying out, the second man jumped up as the table shuddered before his companion's arrival, and he had begun reaching for a shock-pistol which lay on the shelf behind him, when Fisher smashed down the gas bomb on the floor of the room and jerked the door shut, letting fall his own shock-pistol so that he could use both hands to hold the handle and brace backwards against the frantic escape attempt that he anticipated from within.

Shouting between themselves, the two guards arrived at the door. Fisher felt the handle start turning in his grasp and the exertion of strength against his own. The tug-'o-war went on for a moment or two, Fisher holding his own, and after that he heard choking noises from within and the power that strained against him grew less and then stopped its efforts. There was a crash as one of the guards threw a chair through the window on Fisher's right, but the action had been too long delayed, for, as the reddish gas fumes roiled out through the broken glass, he heard both ergo-men slump down into unconsciousness. Then, snatching up his weapon again, Fisher ducked away from all possibility of being gassed himself and passed out through the side door by which Huggins and company had already left the mound, closing up in his wake, and finally he ran to where the others were waiting for him at a safe distance from the doors.

'There you are, Squadron Leader,' he gasped. 'I've given the two guards the quietus with a dose of sleeping gas. We'll hope that's taken care of all the Lexians in there.'

'Hope's very well in its place,' Huggins agreed dryly. 'You can need something more when you're in a jam. Only three of my men are armed.'

'We're not out to kill Lexians,' Fisher warned. 'Our aim is to prevent a war between them and us.'

'There's no deterrent in nine pairs of empty hands,' Huggins reminded.

That much was correct, and it was also true that the Canadians had the right to a means of protecting themselves if the worst came to the worst.

Fisher put his shock-pistol in Huggins' grasp. 'I think I know where I may be able to lay hands on some weapons quickly.'

'You're going back inside?' Huggins asked. 'Isn't there gas floating about in there?'

'I've got a gasmask,' Fisher said, removing it from the pocket of his robe in which he had earlier placed it. 'You fellows stay out here.'

Pulling the mask on, Fisher re-entered the mound. Passing the guardroom, he went straight to the tunnel that opened beyond it, climbed the stairway that led up to the ledge, passed along the rail-protected way until he came to the mouth of the passage that carried the path to the barrack room, and turned left into it, purposing to search the living quarters for the guards' weapons and wondering why it had not occurred to him to do so when he had first entered the room from the ventilation duct. Thus he re-entered the place, and, stepping again over the men who lay senseless on the floor, moved instinctively to a big locker that was isolated against the wall on his right. Opening the locker, he saw inside what he was looking for — about a dozen shock-pistols. The weapons were holstered, and they hung from two parallel lines of pegs. Unhooking the holstered shapes, he piled them up in his arms; then, satisfied that he could more than meet the needs of the men waiting for him out in the night, he left the room, made his way down to ground level, and stepped back outside.

He started walking towards the spot where he had left the Canadians, and was preparing to ask Huggins to come and take some of the weapons from him, when a dazzling light struck him in the eyes and brought him to a standstill. 'This is Doctor Samerle!' rasped a half-familiar voice. 'Empty your hands, Mr. Fisher, and walk straight ahead!'

Fisher let the shock-pistols fall, and kept walking. He had known it for several minutes past. Things had been going too well for him. Now they had gone very wrong indeed.

11

His eyes closed to the tiniest of slits, Fisher went on moving down the brilliant beam of light, and suddenly it snapped out and left him blind and groping; but presently his sight adjusted and he made out the partially lighted shape of a full-sized flying saucer standing about thirty yards beyond him; while between him and it were two groups of figures, one of which was formed by the Canadians and under Lexian armed guard, and the other of which was comprised totally of the aliens and headed by the figure of Doctor Samerle, who now said: 'Better for you that you had died on Lexia, Mr. Fisher. You would have given up your life honouring a sacred trust.'

'As if you care,' Fisher retorted. 'Halshafar was the only failure there.'

'We know who helped you escape from Purna.'

Fisher sensed that Samerle had his suspicions but wasn't sure. 'I helped myself.'

'We know, too, who helped you tonight. And don't imagine that the Emperor has not seen through your purpose.'

Now Fisher was certain that Samerle was fishing. Had there been an admission — or a betrayal — by Hento and Harbiskoom, the doctor's provoking talk would have been unnecessary. 'It takes no great intelligence to see that I meant to take over Project House,' Fisher said.

Samerle glanced at the Canadians. 'So you liberated the few and left the many,' he scorned.

'I couldn't lead a rabble,' Fisher responded glibly. 'We planned to take hostages from among your highly placed. I picked the best men to carry out the task.'

'There could be truth in that,' Samerle muttered. 'But you are throwing sand in my eyes. This is a puerile attempt to blind me to the names of your confederates.'

'I have no confederates. And did such men exist, and you knew who they were, I couldn't possibly hide their names from you.'

'They exist,' Samerle snapped, his tones an admission of his previous trickery. 'You could not have got away from Lexia without the one, or known of what was happening here without the other.'

'I rode home by my own wit,' Fisher lied, 'and I pierced the mound by my own initiative.'

'I do not believe a word of it!' Samerle declared. 'Let us go and see whether Tuga Halshafar is prepared to believe your lies. I must warn you, Mr. Fisher, that he has methods of procuring the truth from false tongues.'

'Should an honest man fear his methods?' Fisher asked.

Samerle made a vicious reply in his own language. Then he issued a string of commands in the same tongue. After that he turned away and led the members of his own group towards the flying saucer. Next an ergo-man detached himself from those watching the Canadians, and, bringing Huggins with him, moved up to

Fisher's back, shock-pistol threatening. Feeling the alien's push, Fisher, too, began walking in the direction of the flying machine, and, as he turned his head and looked across the squadron leader's breasting figure, he saw the other Canadians being driven back towards the mound by the several uniformed men who were still with them.

Leading Huggins and their captor, Fisher climbed the flying machine's steps and entered the control room, where Doctor Samerle and his companions had already taken their seats around the walls. Then, at the doctor's signal, the saucer was sealed and lifted off. It swept briefly through the air at high speed, came to the hover, and then settled earthwards again, landing, as Fisher judged from the pattern of lights that rose to meet it, at the rear of the buildings to the south of Project House.

The machine's door was opened again, and the articulated steps settled into position beneath it. Samerle and company disembarked, and Fisher and Huggins were prodded out behind the men. Fisher saw that the saucer had in fact descended on a lawn that was closer to Project House than he had supposed, and the walk by which they came to the buttress door in the southern side of the granite building was quite a short one.

They passed into the upper corridors of the big house. Here Samerle dismissed the white robed figures with him. Then, beckoning to the prisoners and their guard, he descended the main stairway to the basement, where he led on through the passages until they came to a certain grey door that Hento had shown Fisher before he had set out for the mound. Samerle opened the door, and the captives and their escort moved after him into a large room that contained a daunting array of switchboards, scanners, generators, computers, and electronic equipment generally. Tuga Halshafar stood at the centre of the room's humming, bleep-filled space, and with him were Missenheim, Khaka, and six technicians. The Emperor walked to meet the entrants. He was still wearing his Earth garments, though he had removed his brown contact lenses, and Fisher could not forbear a grimace of amusement at the gasp that Huggins let out as he picked up the strong resemblance between him and Halshafar and began to look rapidly from one to the other. For his part, the Emperor eyed the Earth pair malignantly, then took Samerle aside and began to question him in a low, demanding voice that drew the attention of all present but made no word audible. 'What I'd like to know,' Fisher breathed at Huggins, 'is how they got on to us.'

'The old guy with the crafty face told us,' the squadron leader murmured in reply, 'just after his saucer had dropped out of the sky and nabbed me and my men. There was an open communicator in the guardroom, and — '

There the guard silenced Huggins with a kidney punch. But Fisher had heard all that was necessary. The communicator could only have been the piece of radio equipment that he had seen on the guardroom table out at the mound. The two men on duty there must have been in contact with Project House at the time that the alarm had gone off. Once the bell and the cries of the men had been heard over the air, Samerle's arrival on the scene had undoubtedly been delayed by only as long as it took to summon the saucer, load it with the appropriate men, and fly it to the northern boundary of New Lexia. It had been a stroke of real bad luck. Fisher had a bone-deep feeling that fortune had deserted him completely. One way or another, Huggins and he were as good as dead.

Halshafar spun away from Doctor Samerle. He walked to where Fisher stood and came to a halt before him. His gaze calculated cruelly. 'You have had the help of Harbiskoom, my Lord Chamberlain, and an interplanetary agent named Hento, have you not?'

'I don't believe I even know the gentlemen,' Fisher said.

'We know that you have met Hento,' the Emperor snapped, 'and it seems reasonable to assume that you came in from Lexia with Harbiskoom.'

'I came in from Lexia with a lot of people.'

'Inquiries are being made at the spaceport,' Halshafar warned. 'It will be proved that you and Harbiskoom came in together.'

'Men will say anything for the Emperor, Halshafar.'

'Confirm the guilt of Hento and Harbiskoom, and you shall have an easy death.'

'These two men of whom you speak,' Fisher said — 'should you not be asking them questions?'

The Emperor's face worked.

'You can't find them?' Fisher queried. 'Could that be because they don't exist?'

'We will find them,' the Emperor hissed. 'They cannot be far away.'

'If you will waste your time,' Fisher sighed. 'Doctor Samerle must have told you what my plans were. I was hoping to make you a hostage.'

'You impudent trash!' Halshafar bawled. 'You *will* talk. I have at my command the most agonising method of killing a man. It can be made very slow. I will use it on your companion. His screams will loosen your tongue.'

304

'Tell him what to do with himself,' Huggins advised.

'Halshafar, I can't tell you what I don't know,' Fisher said with a finality that he prayed might be convincing, for he knew that something far more deadly than bluff was coming now.

'In this very room,' the Emperor said, 'I have the means to cook a man from the inside out. The process starts with the frying of his vitals. There is no destruction of the nerve webs in the outer tissues first and the resultant dimming of pain before the centres of the greatest agony are reached. Here the quintessence of pain is experienced from the very beginning of the cooking process. You will smell the vaporising juices of the stomach and lungs before there is any outward sign of damage, and you will see contortions and hear pleas the like of which you have never encountered before. Can you bear to subject a fellow Earthman to that, you scum, while knowing that your own end will be the same?'

'I've said all I can say,' Fisher returned, shuddering inwardly at the word picture that Halshafar had drawn and recalling that, judging from what Morgan of the Home Office had told him in the living room of his far off cottage, the results suggested could be fully achieved. 'I can't believe that the semi-divine ruler of all the Lexians would so degrade himself as to kill by torture two men of a planet from which he may yet have to beg everything. Bad beginnings, Halshafar, make for bad ends.'

'The only ends you need be concerned with,' the Emperor flung back, giving the nod to a technician who had been watching him carefully, 'are those of yourself and the men with you.'

Halshafar faced round. He watched while the technician opened a cupboard and took out three metal objects that looked like jelly moulds. These he set out in the form of a triangle on a piece of open floor close to one of the computers. Then he went to a console within a yard or two of where the Emperor was standing and made some very careful adjustments on the dials present. After that he walked back to the cupboard, took out another of the metal shapes, carried it to the centre of the triangle that he had previously set out, put it down, and then stepped well clear of all the objects on the floor, bowing to Halshafar at the same time; and the Emperor moved to an isolated red switch on the console and pressed it and the metal shape lying at the heart of the triangle trembled and began shrinking, an enormous heat that had obviously started within it working outwards through the metal as a pearly glow which turned it molten and caused it to run glutinously across the floor. Then, slanting his gaze at Fisher, Tuga Halshafar lifted his finger from the switch and said: 'A satisfactory demonstration, I think. Also your last chance.'

'I've repeated myself often enough,' Fisher answered.

'You sound strangely less sure,' the Emperor observed gloatingly, a sign made with his left hand causing two of the technicians to step up to Huggins, pull him forward, and stand him near the puddle of cooling metal at the middle of the triangle. 'Once the switch has made contact, there will be only a moment or so in which to save your fellow's life — though, of course, it may be too late in the first instant after the switch has been pressed.'

Fisher watched Halshafar's hand start to apply pressure. He told himself that it would be in Earth's best interests to let Huggins die — that Harbiskoom and Hento were at present the most valuable of the Lexians and must be kept alive at all costs — but, while also knowing that whatever he said or did not say both he and the squadron leader would almost certainly suffer the fire-blast in the end, Fisher realized that it was not in him to attempt to save even two vitally important aliens by the sacrifice of a brave man of his own kind, and he was about to shout that he would confirm the guilt of Harbiskoom and Hento, when the door opened behind him and the voice of Arle called upon the Emperor to desist.

Halshafar's hand jumped away from the switch, and his face lifted and turned towards the door, frustration causing his lips to compress into an almost invisible line.

'What is this?' Samerle cried. 'You are free, traitor!'

'I am,' Arle agreed, and Fisher twisted his head round and saw the Project Chief holding a shock-pistol on the occupants of the room, while Harbiskoom, Hento, Varinia, and several other Lexians — all likewise armed — were pressing over the threshold at Arle's back. 'The building is ours, sire. All weapons will be dropped to the floor. It is useless to resist us.'

Hysteria burned in Halshafar's eyes. He stabbed a finger at Harbiskoom and screeched: 'I knew you were the enemy, my Lord Chamberlain! I knew — I knew!'

'Yes, I am the enemy,' Harbiskoom agreed. 'I cannot forget the billions of Lexia whom you betrayed. You shall not crown your dishonour by bringing about the final destruction of our race in an unjust war with the peoples of a world to which we come suppliant.'

Shouldering between Huggins — who had stepped out of the triangle and moved back to his former position — and Fisher, the Emperor closed on Harbiskoom, he head thrust forward in vulturine challenge and his hands placed on his hips. 'Poltroon!' he howled, gesturing back at Samerle, Trugel Missenheim, and Khaka. 'There are the real Lexians! What kind of creature are you that you would have us grovel to our inferiors? We are the masters — or nothing! Our greatness gives us the right to rule, and we must enforce our will from the start!'

'We have no possible right to rule on Earth, sire,' Harbiskoom said quietly. 'But we are a great people, and that alone will help us find our place. Is it that you cannot suffer to ask, sire? — or be second best? Pride and ambition were ever the worst follies. How many times did we see it in our own history?' He gazed deeper into the room. 'I would remind my noble peers of that lesson.'

'The very sound of your voice offends!' Halshafar raved; then, seeming about to turn away to the right, he whirled back in the opposite direction and caught Arle's daughter round the middle with his left arm and swung her into the position of a shield, using his right hand to snatch the shock-pistol from her grasp. 'There,' he went on triumphantly, as he sidled towards the room's centre, the struggling Varinia securely held. 'Put down your weapons — all of you: and fast!'

Harbiskoom started forward impulsively. 'Sire, you must think again and — '

Halshafar triggered his shock-pistol. Hit by pale lightning, Harbiskoom fell to the floor and lay with his face pillowed on his crossed forearms.

'Murderer!' Arle shouted; and it seemed that he was about to share the Lord Chamberlain's fate, when Varinia gave her body a serpentine wriggle and put in a tremendous effort to upset the Emperor, the sheer strength of her lithe form taking her out of Halshafar's grasp and causing him to stagger to the rear, his weapon tossed out of line but new murder in his stare.

For a split second everybody in the room, with the exception of the Emperor, was still; then, seeing that the Lexian ruler had steadied up in the triangle and knowing that there was only the one means of averting further tragedy, Fisher threw himself towards the red switch on the console and pressed it, the heat blast again registering unseen at the heart of the three-pointed floor space. Halshafar let out an awful scream, and flung up his arms, steam pouring out of his mouth and the eyes drying up in his head. Then, as heat reddened through the flesh areas visible on him and his skin began to shrivel and his hair to smoke and fall out, Doctor Samerle and Trugel Missenheim tried to grab the man's flailing hands and pull him out of the triangle; but, as they obtained their grips they were also at the limit of their balance, and the Emperor convulsed with an abrupt force that jerked them towards him, and an instant later their screams augmented his own as he literally burst into flames and fired their clothing prematurely. Next, the combined energies of Samerle and the Prime Minister reacting with a kind of cyclonic force, the three of them spun out of the triangle and smashed against the nearby computer, fire catching among the tapes there and then jumping several feet to ignite the fuel in the motors of the generators. Within seconds after that the flames found more sources of combustible material, and the further end of the room was soon engulfed in fire and peopled by blazing and shrieking figures.

There was a rapid retreat from the room by those who were still able. Scorched, but otherwise unhurt, Fisher threw up an arm against the heat and joined it. Checked by the crush in the doorway, he was forced to endure the rapidly rising temperature that much longer than most of the others, and he was close to fainting when Huggins grabbed him under the armpits and dragged him to the back of the passage outside, Arle promptly slamming the door to contain the flames against the appearance of the firefighters for whom Varinia and others were obviously shouting.

'Well done, Fisher,' Huggins said. 'You've fixed it.''

Fisher nodded. He had done precisely that.

It was much later. Arle had summoned Fisher to the council room. Hento was also present. There had been a thorough discussion of the best course that New Lexia could now adopt. It had been agreed that Fisher should go back to England and carry out the role that he had originally been asked to fill: that of the Lexians' intermediary.

Arle had made no apologies for the deception that had been practised on the Earthman in Halshafar's name, and Fisher had asked for none, being determined to keep reproach out of his mind. The past was gone, and there were over three hundred thousand Lexian lives to consider. If Arle had used him, the Project Chief had throughout, and especially after being freed from house arrest by the desperate Harbiskoom and Hento — who had seen nothing for it, when their watch had warned them that something had gone wrong out at the mound, but to attempt a coup of their own — displayed a clear grasp of the realities of the situation. And, as he now said, looking faded and drawn as he sat at the fender-shaped table: 'My time is almost over. It remains only for me to see my people settled. I think it as well that the strong men are all dead, and that I must soon join them. There will be a better chance of peaceful integration between Earthman and Lexian if, on our side, there are no zealots to point out differences of philosophy and custom which really have no importance outside the mind. You must do the best you can on your side, Mr. Fisher.'

'I will plead for tolerance and commonsense,' Fisher promised.

'Thus,' Arle said, stirring uneasily, 'it all lies in the lap of tomorrow.'

But Fisher did not share the old man's fear. Tomorrow was his day.

DEATH CALLED AT NIGHT

R. A. Bennett

Jimmy Ellis believes his parents have died in a car crash when as a young boy he is taken to live with relatives in Australia. The years pass happily, then the nightmare comes. Terrifying images flit through his mind in the dark — all through the eyes of a child, a witness to grisly events seventeen years before. He begins to delve into the past, and soon he finds himself on the trail of a double murderer — a murderer who is prepared to kill again.

THE DEAD TALE-TELLERS

John Newton Chance

Jonathan Blake always kept appointments. He had kept many, in all sorts of places, at all sorts of times, but never one like that one he kept in the house in the woods in the fading light of an October day. It seemed a perfect, peaceful place to visit and perhaps take tea and muffins round the fire. But at this appointment his footsteps dragged, for he knew that inside the house the men with whom he had that date were already dead . . .

THREE DAYS TO LIVE

Robert Charles

Mike Harrigan was scar-faced, a drifter, and something of a woman-hater. With his partner Dan Barton he searched the upper reaches of the Rio Negro in the treacherous rain forests of Brazil, lured by a fortune in uncut emeralds. Behind them rode three killers who believed that they had already found the precious stones. And then fate handed Harrigan not emeralds, but the lives of women, three of them nuns, and trapped them all in a vast series of underground caverns.

TURN DOWN AN EMPTY GLASS

Basil Copper

L.A. private detective Mike Faraday is plunged into a bizarre web of Haitian voodoo and murder when the beautiful singer Jenny Lundquist comes to him in fear for her life. Staked out at the lonely Obelisk Point, Mike sees the sinister Legba, the voodoo god of the crossroads, with his cane and straw sack. But Mike discovers that beneath the superstition and an apparently motiveless series of appalling crimes is an ingenious plot — with a multi-million dollar prize.

DEATH IN RETREAT

George Douglas

On a day of retreat for clergy at Overdale House, a resident guest, Martin Pender, is foully murdered. The primary task of the Regional Homicide Squad is to track down the bogus parson who joined the retreat. Subsequent events show that serious political motives lie behind the killing, but the basic lead to it all is missing. Then, three young tearaways corner the killer in the woods, and a chess problem, set out on a board, yields vital evidence.

THE DEAD DON'T SCREAM

Leonard Gribble

Why had a woman screamed in Knightsbridge? Anthony Slade, the Yard's popular Commander of X2, sets out to investigate. Furthering the same end is Ken Surridge, a PR executive from a Northern consortium. Like Slade, Surridge wants to know why financier Shadwell Staines was shot and why a very scared girl appeared wearing a woollen housecoat. Before any facts can be discovered the girl takes off and Surridge gives chase, with Slade hot on his heels . . .